Cottonwood
By Kevin J. Curtis

Cottonwood
By Kevin J. Curtis

Forward: Research, Accuracy and Historical Fiction

Chapter 1: The Origins of a Monarch

Chapter 2: Reaching for the Sky

Chapter 3: The Quiet Time

Chapter 4: Sinister Visitors

Chapter 5: The Hard Life

Chapter 6: What Comes Around

Chapter 7: Cast of Characters

Chapter 8: What Floated In

Chapter 9: Water, Earth, Sky and the Passage of Time

Chapter 10: Earthen Mounds

Chapter 11: Leaving the Old Behind

Chapter 12: Things Seen and Unseen

Chapter 13: In and Around the Marsh

Chapter 14: Linear Time

Copyright © 2008 by Kevin J. Curtis

Cottonwood
By Kevin J. Curtis

Chapter 15: Storms, Death and New Arrivals

Chapter 16: Outlaws, Robbers and Parasites

Chapter 17: Management and Preservation

Chapter 18: Historical Leftovers

Chapter 19: The "Life" of a Burial

Chapter 20: The "Future" of a Burial Mound

Chapter 21: Anatomy of an Accident

Chapter 22: Inhabitants

Chapter 23: Deadly Finds

Chapter 24: Survival Hunt

Chapter 25: The Hunt

Chapter 26: Making Something from Nothing

Chapter 27: Epilogue

Cottonwood
By Kevin J. Curtis

Forward: Research, Accuracy and Historical Fiction

When I setout to write a historical fiction, I try to make it as historically correct and accurate as possible. This can be quite a challenge when dealing with the past, as the sources often contradict each other.

When I wrote my novel, "He Who Goes First," I had to research an illiterate culture from about eight-hundred years ago. It seemed that even the most reliable sources contradicted all the others. In the end, I had to use what I found to be *most likely*, from as large a group of resources as I could find and manage.

While writing "Cottonwood," I was put into the situation of having to find information about such things as ancient Indian burial mounds. This presented an enormous array of difficulties due to such things as, the sacred nature of the issue to the American Indians, the destruction of sites (over the years) by building, farming, etc., and the looting of grave sites or the archeological practices of the past being somewhat less respectful or inferior to the methodology of today.

It wasn't until 1971 that these burial sites were no longer dug up for "research purposes." It wasn't until 1979 that Minnesota state law, Section 8 of MS 307.08 was passed, that provided for the protection and acquisition of large Indian cemeteries. That left a significant amount of time that these sites were disturbed, damaged and destroyed. What is actually known about them is sometimes difficult to find out because of potential political, spiritual and legal repercussions.

This made my job quite difficult, even though this is largely a work of fiction, and by definition that means that I can take liberties that a nonfiction writer cannot. Still, in my writing of fiction, even if I invent a scenario and characters, I want the event to be accurate in the larger

Cottonwood
By Kevin J. Curtis

historical sense. While I have certainly fabricated a number of vignettes, characters and situations, I have tried to remain as close to "reality" as possible, with my timeline and particulars of the story. This has proven to be quite a task, and I hope any inaccuracies that might be found are minor or open to interpretation.

I have listed a few sources that have helped me formulate my timeline and events, but it is in no way a complete list. Over the years I have read so many publications, books, websites and such, that I have developed a sort of "database" within my own brain that reflects the knowledge of many other sources.

With the topic of the Minnesota River Valley, and particularly the area I'm focusing on, near to and encompassing the Minnesota Valley National Wildlife Refuge, I have a certain intimate knowledge of the landscape and wildlife due to my years of hiking these areas as a volunteer park ranger. I have been in all of the refuge units and much of the surrounding public land adjacent to it. I have hiked the established trails, and gone on foot, off-trail into some pretty rugged terrain.

There are such hazards as sinking mud, biting insects and poisonous or thorny plants that I have dealt with. I have had confrontations with animals both wild and domestic and also people who were using the land illegally. I have found things (including nests or land and water features) that the (Minnesota Fish & Wildlife Service) staff was unaware of, because they do not travel on foot to the extent that I have.

I have ventured into these areas repeatedly, in all seasons and in all types of weather. Such repeated activity and continuous research of what I have witnessed and found, has both given me (I think) a unique perspective of this huge area of land and water, as well as the realization that nature and the animals don't always follow the "rules"

Cottonwood
By Kevin J. Curtis

established by those who write books about them. My thought is that perhaps these animals haven't read the books and don't know any better.

In the end, I hope that this novel can give the reader a glimpse into a unique and wondrous place that has given me hours, days, and years of solitude, time to reflect and true joy. At a time when I was feeling depressed about my "lot in life," I had two Bald Eagles soar just over my head while in Louisville Swamp. I can still remember the quiet sound of the wind going through their wings. I decided at that particular moment in time, that I was truly blessed.

Copyright © 2008 by Kevin J. Curtis

Cottonwood
By Kevin J. Curtis

Chapter 1: The Origins of a Monarch

     The wind was strong as it blew across the bottomland forest of the Minnesota River Valley. A funnel formed and it sucked the cattails upward as it moved along the marsh. It would have been most impressive… had there been anyone there to see it. The miniature tornado continued to cross the marsh and then it passed over the creek and crashed into a stand of trees. It lost its momentum as it hit a giant Cottonwood tree that had grown near the creek for almost a century. The mighty tree tamed the wind funnel and it emerged from the woods as merely a strong breeze.

     The Cottonwood stood over ninety feet tall,[1] and it had a trunk that was five feet in diameter.[2] Cottonwood trees can be either male or female, and this old lady was in the late stages of her life. It was late spring, and the trademark cotton was blowing from her, carrying the seeds of the next generation of trees. The seeds were minute in comparison to the giant that they had come from. The wind carried them easily across the marsh and through the forest. They sailed over the river and then filled the sky like a white cloud.

     One seed flew over the river, and then hovered over a small stream as the wind current stalled temporarily. The seed seemed to be watching the snapping turtle below. The large turtle had been traveling down the small stream when it found itself falling over a small waterfall that was hidden amongst the tall grass and cattails. The turtle had fallen about two and a half feet to the bottom.[3] As the armored amphibian began to orient itself, the wind shifted and the seed was carried away.

     It flew on across the Minnesota River and landed at the edge of a clearing near a marsh. A short distance away, an outcropping of stone jutted out from a bluff that outlined

Cottonwood
By Kevin J. Curtis

the edge of the swamp. A creek wound its way along the edge of the bluff before emptying into the marsh. Another stream carried the overflow into the swamp–which in turn emptied into the river. In short, the diversity of the landscape was impressive. There were trees, prairie, and wetlands all in close proximity. The tiny seed had found a resting place in this vast ecosystem. The fibers of the white cotton stuck to the rich soil that was made up of decaying plant material. The dampness soon affected the seed and with the warmth of the sun, it began to germinate.

    This land was occupied by many living things, and among them, were human beings. The end of one era had come, and a new one was just now emerging. The American Indians had occupied this land for thousands of years, and a young warrior ran close to where the seed had begun to grow. Unknowingly, the young man dropped to the ground, just inches from the tiny cottonwood. He was injured. There was blood dripping from his arm. Down his hand, several drops fell from his fingertips and landed on the new tree. The warrior scooped some of the soft mud from the ground, and packed it against the wound on his arm. He succeeded in stopping the bleeding. He rose to his feet and continued on his journey.

    The drops of blood had soaked into the black soil that the young tree was taking root in. Slowly, the tree used a small portion of the blood droplets as food to nourish it. In this way, the Indian had become part of the young cottonwood. Though the warrior had now left the area, his blood had become part of the growing life within the tree. The following morning, the first tiny leaf would begin to form.

    The young warrior ran on. He ignored the pain of his wound and hurried along, trying to put as much distance between himself and his assailants as possible. He had been hunting for small game, when he had wandered into the

Cottonwood
By Kevin J. Curtis

vicinity of another group of young American Indians. They exchanged greetings, and then the others jumped the young man, intent on stealing the contents of his deerskin bag that was over his shoulder.

The fight had been brief, but one of the three assailants had managed to slice open the young warrior's forearm with a knife before he was able to escape. The three gave chase, but the young man was pumped up on adrenaline, was thin and he was fast. Though he had already outrun his pursuers, he kept going–not wanting to take any chances that they might catch up to him.

The river valley was ancient, and the laws of nature governed it. One force that dominated the landscape was of course the Minnesota River. The river wound back and forth within the confines of the valley it had created. It was a beautiful and sometimes deadly environment.

On certain occasions, usually a couple of times each year, the river broke free of the huge depression it had carved. After the winter ice broke, as the snow from the surrounding land melted, the water rushed through ancient gullies into the river that would swell under the sheer volume of water. Eventually, the river would break free of the banks that usually kept it in check, and it would spill back over the sides and flood the lowlands of the bottomland forest.

Frequently, at some point during the spring or summer, heavy rains could have the same effect. This was most impressive after an extended dry spell, when the parched ground could not absorb the heavy rain fast enough. The water flowed across the dry ground, spilling into the river until it swelled over its banks.

Sometimes the quantity of water was unfathomable. To rise up, filling vast portions of the valley took such a huge amount, that it seemed impossible. Yet, the snowmelt, rain and the river had repeated this cycle over such a vast

Cottonwood
By Kevin J. Curtis

span of time that it was just as unfathomable and seemed equally impossible that anything could be so old.

The tiny tree faced a variety of hazards. As it stretched toward the sunlight, other, faster growing plants competed for space and nutrients. As the full warmth of summer set in, the rising temperature and wind began to dry the ground. The small tree was only rooted to the surface of the soil and the lack of moisture began to stress the fragile plant. Fortunately, a storm thundered through the river valley and drenched the parched earth.

These storms and floods gave life to the trees and plants in this ecosystem. Ironically, these same floods and storms destroyed just as readily as they gave. While this tiny tree benefited from the storm, the winds and the ground that was loosened by the rains felled others. The little tree absorbed the moisture and grew stronger. Unfortunately, the surrounding plants also grew stronger and larger and they began to shade the struggling tree.

Late one evening as the last rays of daylight faded behind the bluffs, a group of White-tailed Deer wandered into the area where the tiny cottonwood struggled for survival. The animals browsed the growing foliage, and devoured leaves, stems and grass. If one grabbed hold of the tiny morsel of a tree, its short life would be completed. As fate would have it, the deer moved through and one ate the grass and plants that surrounded the tiny tree. As its hoofed feet came dangerously close to stepping on, and crushing the tree, it moved away with the rest of the group. The animals stayed in the area for awhile, and continued to feed on the vegetation before moving off into the night.

When morning came, the little tree was no worse for the close encounter with the deer. In fact, it was no longer shaded by the thick growth that had previously surrounded it. The deer had also left droppings in the area that were soon decayed by insects and bacteria and

Cottonwood
By Kevin J. Curtis

absorbed into the soil. The nutrients from the deer waste were incorporated into the tiny tree as it used this for food. Conditions were excellent for the tree, and though the deer were now gone, they had become part of the life-force of the small cottonwood.

Life in the river valley was made up of the individual life form's ability to adapt and survive, as well as a good dose of luck in the type of conditions that existed in its environment. This little tree had avoided many potential hazards, while it was able to utilize the available nutrients, moisture and sunlight to continue its growth toward becoming a monarch of the bottomland forest.

The odds were stacked against the tree from making it to maturity. While thousands of seeds were released by the cottonwood trees each spring, only a tiny fraction of them actually germinated, and even less ever made it to the enormous size that was potentially theirs.

The cottonwoods did not usually possess the deep rings of wood characteristic of many hardwoods. As a matter-of-fact, when these softwoods did reach maturity, they were usually quite hollow inside. This made the giant trees perfect homes for many wild animals and birds. Frequently the initiators of this process were the woodpeckers.

A variety of woodpeckers filled the bottomland forest. Their distinctive calls were heard during any season. These were the year-round, resident "workmen" that carved holes into the trees. This opened the access to the relative safety of the hollows inside. The cottonwoods were especially useful for nesting places. A huge tree could house a vast array of birds, mammals and insects.

Cottonwood
By Kevin J. Curtis

Chapter 2: Reaching for the Sky

In June of that year, the drought of the previous season was finally broken. Rains were hard and frequent and the river began to rise quickly. Fortunately, for the small cottonwood, it had by now, produced a root system that held it in place when the river finally washed over its banks.

Some of the trees growing near the river's edge were washed out by the current and they fell. Some landed in the river and were pulled downstream by the torrent. Other trees were too heavy to be supported by the saturated ground. The wind and floodwaters pulled many down. Still, there was an abundance of trees and growth. The floodwaters carried a layer of silt and mud from the river and deposited the rich soil onto the forest floor.

The small cottonwood tree clung to the soil as it was eroded and replaced by mud. Though the tree was nearly completely submerged by the floodwaters, it survived until the waters began to recede. As the river returned to the confines of its banks, the erosion of the edges was evident. The land and water had exchanged form and fluid in the process. While some of the forest floor was washed away, the white residue on the foliage and the thick mud remained behind. The cottonwood was now surrounded by the nutrient rich muck left over by this union.

As the foliage grew through the mud and fallen trees, the traces of the flooding were quickly disappearing from sight. The small tree kept growing quickly both downward as its roots dug into the soil, and upward as its leaves reached for the sunlight above.

When July arrived, the weather became hot and dry. Soon, there was a haze in the air, which was a mixture of high humidity and smoke. The grasslands were on fire, and

Cottonwood
By Kevin J. Curtis

some of the forest was also burned. The damage was a mixed blessing. Though a number of animals were killed and many trees were destroyed, the fire was also beneficial. Behind the destruction, there was rich soil and a "blank canvas" for the wilderness to paint its new growth on.

Around the forest, the animals were busily living their lives within the heat of the summer. Some were hiding bits of food for use during the long coming winter. All were busily eating and putting on weight before the fall forced them to migrate to warmer climates or the winter's cold and snow reduced the available food supply.

The wilderness was filled with new life. The woods showed off colors of bellflowers, coneflowers and columbine. The prairie had such showy flowers as Butterfly weed, Prairie Smoke, vervain and more.

The resident animals were raising their young. High above the forest floor, a young bald eagle sat in its nest. It hadn't learned to fly yet, but it was actively stretching and flapping its wings. Periodically, the eagle parents would fly in after fishing to feed it. The young bird and its parents called out, in a metallic screech that echoed out into the four directions.

The American Indians believed that the eagles were the closest to the Creator, since they could fly high above the Earth with little effort. The Native Americans found value in the animals and plants that lived here, and they knew that these things allowed them to survive. The new human immigrants, who traveled across the great waters were less reverent and often saw the frontier as something to be conquered. The idea of the significance of the four winds and the four directions was lost on them. They sought to "tame" the wilderness and plant gardens and fence off portions of the land to contain their livestock. It was inevitable that the interlopers and the indigenous peoples would develop an uneasy relationship as the white-

Cottonwood
By Kevin J. Curtis

skinned newcomers built their homes on the Indians' ancestral lands.

The newcomers looked at the natives as "savages," who were in need of "saving." This was because the indigenous people were not baptized, and had not devoted their lives to Christ. The Indians saw the Europeans as intrusive, and wanting to change all that the Creator had given them. Although the Indians were spiritual and believed in a powerful Creator, and the Whites believed in God and Christ the Savior, neither could at that point in time, believe that perhaps God and the Creator were one-in-the-same.

In the bluffs above, the scream of a cougar lofted down on the breeze. The cat was announcing its possession of this territory. The deer within earshot were frozen by the sound. Their tails rose instinctively showing the white underside. Their ears flicked nervously as they assessed their proximity to the danger.

A black bear ambled by, largely unaffected by the cat's bold announcement. Squirrels sat chattering softly from the safety of the trees. The entire forest was alive, and the wildflowers bloomed in spectacular colors in the prairie nearby.

Late in the summer, many plants had gone to seed. The sparrows had finished raising their second set of offspring and the young birds were now on their own. The sun was lower in the sky, and that meant less sunlight. This was a major triggering mechanism for many plants and animals that the warm season was coming to a close.

The cottonwood had grown into a small "whip" of a tree by summer's end. It had passed the first test on its way to becoming a full-fledged monarch of the bottomland forest. As the weather cooled and the sunlight waned, the cottonwood joined the other trees of the forest as they dropped their leaves onto the moist ground.

Cottonwood
By Kevin J. Curtis

The leaves of many of the trees and plants were brilliant in color. The previous greens and browns were now replaced by a dazzling array of yellows, oranges and reds. The greens were still present, though many of the formerly green grasses and plants were brown and dried now that the fall season had set in.

Winter was coming, and that meant big changes to the forest and the animals that lived there. Some would go dormant and sleep through the frozen months, tucked safely away inside of snug burrows. Others would live off the food they stored up during the summer and fall months. Still others would be at the mercy of the elements and what scarce food was to be found amidst the ice, snow and driving wind.

The wind howled angrily as the temperature began to drop. The rain that was driven by the wind began to turn into ice. Soon the trees and land were covered by a slick coating of frozen rain. The limbs and branches of the trees and plants were burdened by the weight of the ice. Some lost branches under the stress of the weight. Late in the night as the storm gained in fury, the white of new fallen snow began to brighten up the landscape. Beneath this snow, near the small cottonwood tree, was one of the victims of the storm. A chickadee had succumbed to the freezing rain. Its frozen body lay lifeless beneath the snow.

Cottonwood
By Kevin J. Curtis

Chapter 3: The Quiet Time

The next few months would find the small tree in dormancy. Its life was no less in jeopardy, as hungry rabbits, mice and other animals devoured the available plant material to eek out their meager subsistence during the winter months. These animals in return, were hunted relentlessly by the resident predators, who also found more difficulty locating prey.

The marsh was now freezing over, and the beavers and muskrats were kept busy keeping their air holes open. Their lodges afforded protection from the elements and predators–especially once the wood-and-mud lodges froze solid. The opening into these lodges was beneath the surface of the water, and when the top froze over, most predators did not have the strength or determination to open them up.

That did not stop the coyote, who had planted himself at the open air hole on the frozen ice of the marsh pond. The wild dog was motionless, yet poised to strike. This was an experienced animal that knew the key to success was in staying motionless. A few minutes went by… then almost an hour. Suddenly, without warning the coyote jumped at the opening and tossed a fat muskrat onto the ice.

The coyote jumped on its prey and then jubilantly tossed it high into the air. The rodent hit the ice with a small thud and before it could regain its senses, the coyote held it down with its front paws and tore it in half. The muskrat was gone in two gulps. The coyote moved on, temporarily satisfied.

Above, a Red-tailed Hawk soared over the marsh. It continued on, making ever-higher circles that gradually moved off toward a clearing. The hawk was looking for food. Its sharp eyes searched for minute movements in the

Cottonwood
By Kevin J. Curtis

snow. Such a thing would cause it to plunge downward with deadly talons.

Bows in hand, two young Indian boys were running silently through the forest on an ancient trail. The trail was created by the shared use of deer, humans and various other travelers. The flight of the hawk did not go unnoticed, as the boys slowed to watch the bird overhead. Its auburn-red tail feathers shown as it angled in flight against the rays of sunlight. The Indians believed that the hawk was a messenger from the world beyond. If the great bird had a message for them, they were going to pay attention.

The hawk banked against the air current and vanished out of sight. The boys continued on their way looking for suitable game to help support their hungry families. Life was challenging in the river valley, and it was necessary to be diligent in the search for food whether one was man or beast. Not far from here, the women of the tribe were busy drying food and preparing it for the long cold season.

Gliding on their bellies, a family of otters was having fun sliding down the embankment into the still-open river nearby. Their squeaks betrayed the delight they were having in the snow and mud. The cold didn't seem to affect them as they slid into the water and disappeared. Their well-oiled fur and a layer of fat kept them insulated from the river's chill.

Above in the cottonwood trees there was a small group of Bald Eagles. The eagles became sociable during the winter, though they could be quite territorial during the breeding season. These huge birds controlled the sky and hunted both the land and water. They were notorious scavengers and thieves. While more than able to hunt for food on their own, they were as likely to steal a meal from an osprey or other more ambitious hunter. The eagles preferred fish, but were opportunistic and sometimes fed on

Cottonwood
By Kevin J. Curtis

carrion too.

Now as the winter season had set in, the group was easily visible in the tall trees. The older birds had the white heads and tails that appeared after about four seasons. The younger birds were brown-headed and had white speckles–especially underneath their huge wings. There were fewer other hunters to pilfer food from now, and the eagles had to rely on fishing the parts of the river that remained open, as well as scavenging. As the river began to freeze over and less and less of it was open, the eagles congregated in larger groups near the areas of still open water. If the temperature continued to drop, they might need to fly further to the south to find open water.

A large Tundra Swan swam solo in the open river. The other swans had migrated through this area weeks earlier. They had stopped in the marsh for a couple of weeks to rest and feed before continuing their journey southward. They had been at their breeding grounds in the tundra of northern Canada over the warm season. This single bird had been unable to continue the migration and was now left to fend for itself. It was obviously unnerved by the close proximity of the band of eagles, though it was also reliant on the open water to survive. The large white bird's survival was in jeopardy. It was unlikely to make it through the season. The death of such a large bird, however, would provide life-sustaining nourishment for others in this time of scarcity.

Close by, a large Black Bear was digging under the roots of a huge cottonwood tree. The bear was fattened on acorns, sedges, insects and numerous other delicacies. It was time now to settle in for the winter hibernation. This state of sleep, combined with the lowering of its metabolism to a point that would barely sustain its life, allowed this large omnivore to survive through the lean winter months. By spring, it would be thinner and ready to

Cottonwood
By Kevin J. Curtis

begin the feasting all over again.

The weather continued to grow colder and the snow continued to fall. The woods took on a silence as the snow filled the air and blanketed the ground. Off in the distance, a Pileated Woodpecker hammered against a tree as it searched for insects beneath the bark. These were the "workmen" of the forest. The holes they chiseled into the trees opened up the cavities that supported a variety of wildlife.

An elk bugled in the distance, and the sounds of wolves howling, came from across the river. These were some of the animals that would be forever lost to this place, once the human beings from Europe, Africa and Asia moved into the North American Continent with greater frequency.

For now, the woods took on a quiet, white grandeur. The cold set in and the inhabitants of the bottomland forest held on to life as best as they could. Some wouldn't survive. That was the reality of life. Those that were strong, prepared, or lucky would make it through to the spring.

The jackrabbit turned white and blended into the snow. With each powerful leap, this hare could cover twenty feet.[4] The White-tailed Deer were foraging for food as best as they could. If observant, a person could notice the absence of plant material between the surface of the ground and as high as the deer could reach. If the winter was severe, many of the deer might starve. Fortunately, the death of one of these animals would provide food for many others. This was the fate of one elderly doe.

The doe had been part of a larger group of deer, but she was having difficulty keeping up with the rest of the herd. Breathing heavily, she stopped, unable to continue. The other deer lingered momentarily, but they were driven on by the need to find food. Weakened, and separated from the group, the doe struggled to find food in the deep snow.

Cottonwood
By Kevin J. Curtis

Before long, she was forced to lie down and conserve her remaining strength.

It didn't take too long, before a hungry Mountain Lion came down into the bottomland looking for just such a likely meal as a weakened deer could make. The cat didn't bother to be stealthy, as it knew the deer was dieing. You could hear the intermittent screams of the lone male cougar, as it followed the scent of the weakened doe. When the big cat was within sight, the doe left her hiding place and tried one last burst of speed to escape.

The puma was in pursuit though, and it was only a few moments before he launched himself onto the neck and shoulders of the frightened deer. The doe tried to run, but the power and weight of the cougar dragged her down. Finding the throat of the exhausted deer, the cat closed his jaws over it and the mighty fangs of the feline severed the carotid artery and opened the throat. The deer kicked briefly as its breath mixed with its blood. Then there was silence.

The cougar used its rough tongue to lick the hair off of the deer hide. It used its sharp teeth and powerful jaws to tear hunks of flesh off of the deer carcass. When he had eaten a significant portion of the deer, the cougar dragged the remaining carcass out of the open and into the scrub brush. With any luck, there might be a few frozen pieces of meat remaining if the large cat came by here again within the next few days.

With all of the hungry animals this time of year, the likelihood that much would be left was low. Even now, a number of onlookers were biding their time from treetops or other hiding places. Once the cougar left his prize and moved on, there would be a race to see which of the scavengers would move in first.

Being first might guarantee a portion, but there would also be the inevitable confrontations between

Cottonwood
By Kevin J. Curtis

competing animals. A deer carcass was worth fighting for, though few would risk being killed for such a thing–even in the dead of winter. There was both a need to eat, and a need to conserve energy during the lean months.

<u>Chapter 4: Sinister Visitors</u>

     As the last remnants of winter attempted to hang on, the sun began to burn higher in the sky. The added sunlight and more direct rays began to warm the bottomland forest. First to open was the Minnesota River. The current and water runoff weakened the thin ice, and soon the movement of the water was pushing the ice sheets into the bank. The sound of the ice breaking was almost like shattering glass, except it seemed to go on and on forever.

     As the snow began to melt off, the buds of the trees were visible as they readied themselves to burst open in an explosion of green life. The animals were becoming more active, and those that were safe in their winter burrows were waking up and growing restless. There were other more sinister changes going on as well.

     Two men on horseback rode into the valley. A mule was in tow, and on its back, there was something wrapped inside of old burlap bags. The two men were newcomers to this area, and they had just come from one of the new farms just a few miles away. They were here in the river valley to hide something that they had done.

     The two men were brothers and they had arrived from Europe less than two years earlier. They had had a drunken dispute with a neighbor, which ended tragically. They had not meant to kill the man, but now that they had, they needed to find a remote place to dispose of the body.

     They rode to the riverbank alongside of the marsh. The mule came dangerously close to walking on the new cottonwood tree as it carried its burden along. The tree was

Cottonwood
By Kevin J. Curtis

still a small whip, but the mule with its load was heavy enough to do serious damage. Fortunately, the animal's hooves narrowly missed the young tree.

The men stopped along the river and looked around to see if they were alone. Reassured that no one was nearby they untied the tethers and removed the corpse from the back of the mule. They dropped it to the ground unceremoniously, and began to climb down the edge of the riverbank in search of large stones. The bank was muddy, and it took several minutes for them to heave the rocks up to the top of the bank.

They secured the rocks in two burlap bags, and tied one around the neck of the corpse and the other around the ankles. Then, they heaved the body over the bank and watched as it sank into the dark water of the river as a fountain of bubbles came to the surface.

They were muddy and tired, but the job had been done. Now they need only ride back to their farm and live the lie that they had no knowledge of the recent disappearance of their neighbor. They climbed back onto their horses and led the mule back out the way they had come.

Later that evening, a small group of three American Indians stopped near the cottonwood tree. They were nearing their objective for this night and wanted to go over the plan of action.

One brave began by saying that the "fat-eaters" were living just beyond the forest. They would go to the white people's homes and steal some of their livestock. The Indians did not like the fact that the white settlers had moved in and put up fences across the land. The indigenous people were nomadic and did not believe in the concept that a person could own the land.

Disputes were not uncommon between the newcomers and the Native Americans. Regardless of this,

Cottonwood
By Kevin J. Curtis

there was also trade between the two groups. Still there was often an uneasiness and lack of trust between the Europeans and the Indians.

Just as dark set in, the Indians moved silently onto the farm and they took several chickens. The birds were startled and began to make a racket that was noticed by the pair of farm dogs. The dogs gave chase and the Indians ran with the stolen birds. The two brothers and their families who lived on this farm were alerted and the two men grabbed their guns and began shooting at the Indians. The interlopers fired back and the shooting caused the dogs to give up their chase.

As the natives ran away with the stolen chickens, the two farmers came to an uneasy realization. They had suspected their neighbor had stolen livestock from them and had confronted him with deadly results. Now, as this same neighbor's body was anchored by rocks to the bottom of the river, the two brothers realized that they might have made a ghastly mistake. The thought that they had murdered an innocent man weighed heavily on them as they solemnly returned to the house with their excited families.

When the Indians returned to their village with the stolen chickens, not everyone was pleased. This action could provoke the whites, who were well armed. Though there were fewer of them than there were Indians in the area, such an altercation could bring the army down on them. This had happened to other tribes. The three braves remained defiant and boasted that they could kill the entire army by themselves. The War Chief was unimpressed by the young bucks. He had seen many battles and he was aware of the power of the white army.

"You may have brought danger to us all!" he scolded. "You will not do such a thing again!

Cottonwood
By Kevin J. Curtis

* * * *

It was that volatile period of the early spring. One day might be warm and sunny, and the next day could be blowing with snow or freezing rain. Today was pleasant, with just a hint of warmth on a light breeze. The fog had been burning off slowly as the morning sun grew stronger in the east.

The remaining snow was confined to the shadows. Ice remained below the surface of the beaver pond, but occasionally a chunk would break free and float to the surface where it dazzled in the sunlight until it melted away into liquid water. The sun was strong in the sky now, and the fog was disappearing fast.

The birds were busily readying themselves for the new day, and the new season. Flocks of ducks crossed the morning sky in "V" formations. Nearby a Swamp Sparrow was trying to court females with his song. He had returned from a more southern climate, and was now staking out his breeding territory.

The bird had positioned himself atop of a pussy willow bush, with a grand view of the woods and swamp. He was master of his domain, and ready to attract a mate for the new season. The instinctive drive to nest was strong in both the male and female. A diligent, hardworking pair could raise at least two broods in a season.

The sparrow repeated his call over and over, hoping to gain attention. He had survived the winter, migration, and all was well in his world now. The day was brightening every minute that he was singing, and the joy came through in the little bird's voice.

If any intruders arrived within the confines of his territorial boundaries, he flew at them and drove the interlopers away. He had found the ideal location to find a mate and build a nest.

Copyright © 2008 by Kevin J. Curtis

Cottonwood
By Kevin J. Curtis

Suddenly, and without warning, a missile flew down from the sky and hit the sparrow square. He had not seen the Peregrine Falcon, which was the speedster of the bird world. Death came quickly to the sparrow and also for his dreams of finding a female and raising young.

The falcon was passing through, looking for new territory of its own. This raptor was hungry, and the sparrow perched on top of the pussy willow bush was too tempting to pass up. The falcon flew high into a large cottonwood and began tearing off chunks of its prey and swallowing them whole. When it had finished eating what it wanted, it left the less desirable pieces fall to the ground below. Satisfied, the peregrine continued on its way.

Chapter 5: The Hard Life

The mink swam to the shore of the marsh pond with a fish in its mouth. It was a Yellow Perch. The mink sat on the bank and crunched through the fish's scales and into the nutrient rich flesh beneath. As the weather began to warm, the bottomland forest teamed with life.

A lone wolf trotted through the marsh at dusk. The coyotes noticed it, but they were not going to attempt to attack a healthy wolf. Though it was not sick, this wolf was growing old. He had lived for seven seasons, and had risen to lead his pack for the last four. Then, a younger male was finally able to drive the elder away. Had he not left the pack, he would probably have died in the fight.

It had been a brief yet fierce battle. This old wolf still carried the scars of the altercation. There was no true malice in what had taken place. It was simply the natural order of things. Four years earlier, this wolf had challenged the dominant male for supremacy and had claimed his victory and the right to lead the pack.

Wolves don't live long, and the claim to leadership

Cottonwood
By Kevin J. Curtis

was fleeting. This wolf had become too old to maintain control of his pack and now he wandered the forest alone. He trotted on, out of sight.

A Leopard Frog sat motionless, floating in the shallow water of the pond. It had gorged itself on insects and was now at rest. A huge Garter Snake swam through the pond and it noticed the frog. Just before the snake struck, the frog kicked its large legs and swam away from the snake. This was what happened most often when a predator pursued its prey. The success rate for most of the predators was not good. These animals had to balance the energy they expended with the energy gained by a successful kill. Therefore, the snake did not continue to pursue the frog.

In the marsh pond, a large beaver made its way underwater along the bank. As it began to crawl up the submerged bank, there was a snap and the beaver felt a sharp pain as a metal trap closed on its front leg. It pulled against the cruel metal, but the teeth dug into the animal's leg and the spring held it tight.

The trap was set under water, and the beaver was held below the surface. In an ironic twist of fate, the animal that was so much at home in the water, now held its breath for the last time. Several minutes went past. Then more time went by. Eventually the beaver was unable to hold its breath any longer. It instinctively took in a breath and as its lungs filled with water, it kicked furiously against the trap. Then it was still.

High above in the treetops, a Red Squirrel stopped its chattering and listened intently. Off in the distance there was a faint sound of vicious growls and squeals. The lone wolf had wandered into the territory of the resident wolf pack. The pack converged on the interloper and after a couple of minutes, the sound stopped. The old wolf was killed and his throat was torn open by the teeth of his own

Cottonwood
By Kevin J. Curtis

kind. The squirrel ran off to continue its life.

The next day, an American Indian walked along the marsh pond. He stopped, and reached down into the water where he found a chain secured to a wooden stake. He pulled on the chain and it came up with a drowned beaver held by its foreleg in a metal jaw trap. The Indian removed the carcass and reset the trap. He put the beaver in his pack and continued on toward his next trap.

Higher up the bluffs, a white man waited in the shadows of a tree. He had covered his human scent by rubbing his clothes with raccoon urine. It was a tactic used by hunters. Raccoons were common and easy enough to trap. They were not the normal food of most of the dangerous predators, nor were they particularly dangerous except for very small animals, birds and fish. Because of this, the scent of a raccoon would not cause any undue concern for the animals the man was hunting.

Nearby was part of a deer carcass. The man was waiting in ambush. After a few hours, he found what he was waiting for; or rather, they had found the deer leftovers. The three wolves came slowly, but the smell of the deer meat was powerful. They finally moved closer. One bold wolf finally moved over to the carcass and began to rip a chunk loose and then it swallowed the piece whole. Another wolf inched closer, and was immediately rebuffed by the first.

The retreating wolf was suddenly grabbed by a jaw trap that was carefully hidden near the deer carcass. The powerful spring slammed the vicious teeth of the trap into the animal's rear leg, down to the bone. The wolf let out a startled squeal and then began to fight against the trap. Its predicament and reaction caused the other two wolves to forget the deer carcass. Just before they could retreat, a shot rang out and the first wolf dropped to the ground as the bullet crashed through its side and into its lung.

Cottonwood
By Kevin J. Curtis

The third wolf sprang into the woods and disappeared as the hunter broke from his cover and moved in. He shot again and finished off the wolf that was lying in its own blood. Then the man grabbed a pistol from his waistband and as he moved toward the wolf in the trap, the wild canine bristled and showed its teeth and its combined fear and displeasure. The man smiled and pulled back the hammer of his gun. He pointed it at the wolf's head and pulled the trigger.

* * * *

The Scotsman chewed the stub of a cigar in the corner of his mouth. His gut was enormous and protruded to such an extent that he could not see his own feet. He wandered around, bad-tempered and most who met him were careful not to cross him.

The Scotsman had a patch covering one eye, which made him appear even more formidable. One could tell that this man knew both hardship and also excess. His establishment sat near to the river, and it served many functions. It was a trading post, where one could find supplies, food, whiskey, and maybe even women for sale. It was also, where the trappers brought their furs in exchange for money or goods.

Outside, two boys were busily packing furs into bundles for the journey to civilization. Most of what the Scotsman took in was furs, though he was not averse to trading anything that might prove valuable. He considered himself a businessman, and he kept a good supply of whiskey, gunpowder, knives, jerky and other supplies that his customers would want.

Close by a flock of Canadian Geese was swimming in the river. The adults were outnumbered by the little "fluff-balls" that followed them. There were six adults and twenty-seven young. As they made their way along the river's edge, one of the goslings at the rear of the group

Cottonwood
By Kevin J. Curtis

disappeared. Then another went under and didn't come up. Eventually, the group made its way onto land, where none of them seemed to notice that only twenty-five goslings remained.

With large fish and large turtles in the river, it was a dangerous place for the new geese–not that the land would afford them much more protection. As the flock moved onto the bank and began to graze on the short grass, a Red Fox watched from the distant brush. It licked its mouth and continued waiting.

In a short time to come, the over hunting by man would reduce the numbers of the Canada Geese until they nearly became extinct. This would happen to a number of species as the Europeans brought their technology and their hatred of predators and tendency toward overuse of the environment.

Fortunately, in the case of the Canada Geese as a whole, a small population would exist in the north of Canada. Eventually some enlightened people would enact laws for the protection of endangered species and they would make a remarkable comeback. That time was still far-off though.

Man, as a species still did not have either the knowledge or the resources to make such a bold change. At the time, it seemed that there was a never-ending supply of wilderness and wild animals, and that these should be conquered. It wasn't until human beings reached the point where they were not continuously working to provide for their family's next meal, that they could concern themselves with the welfare of the other animals that shared the Earth with them.

The geese became agitated, and led their goslings away, still under the watchful eyes of the fox. A birch-bark canoe pulled up to the shore and two Indians got out, pulled the canoe up, and then began to unload its contents.

Cottonwood
By Kevin J. Curtis

Rawhide straps tethered the bundles of furs, and the two men heaved the loads onto their backs and walked up toward the trading post.

The Scotsman saw them coming, and he met the two Indians outside. It was not his being polite, so much as he didn't want them to come inside. He motioned for them to drop their bundles onto a nearby table. The two men did as they were asked, and the Scotsman began to look at the furs they had brought.

He shook his red face back and forth and scowled. He was not pleased by the quality of the merchandise. The Indians knew their furs were high quality, and they soon became upset. The Scotsman moved his huge body through the doorframe and returned with more traps, a knife and a jug of whiskey.

The Indians obviously wanted more, but they eyed the Scotsman suspiciously. Finally, one of them burst out in anger, which was met by an equivalent response by the Scotsman. Eventually, the Scotsman went inside once more and returned with a mirror, a metal pot and another smaller jug of whiskey. He slammed the goods down with much authority, and pointed the Indians back toward their canoe.

By this time, the two boys had ceased their work packing bundles of furs, and they each had a scattergun pointed toward the two Indians. Seeing this, the two trappers returned to their canoe and paddled off.

Sometime later, two white men showed up at the trading post. They were invited in by the Scotsman, who poured them each a shot of whiskey before continuing the conversation. The trappers displayed their furs, and again, the Scotsman scowled. He pointed to the furs that the Indians had just brought, that the two boys were now going through.

"These here," he said as he grabbed a fine beaver pelt, "these are high-quality furs! What ye' have there

Cottonwood
By Kevin J. Curtis

lads… doesn't match up!"

The two men protested, and the Scotsman played his little game, finally becoming angry and giving the men more than he apparently had intended. In the end, the trappers wandered off with their goods, feeling the effects of the whiskey.

The Scotsman knew the pelts were good; at least for summertime. Everyone knew that a winter coat was thicker and more plush than a summer-killed fur. Still, he wasn't about to send them away, since ninety-percent of his business revolved around the fur trade. People back east and in Europe were crazy about the furs that came out of the west. All kinds of animals were taken for their warm furry coats, but it was perhaps the beaver that did more for the economy and the expansion of the west than all the others combined. It was fortunate that the large rodents were as prolific as they were industrious.

Nearby, the fox finished the last bit of gosling that had made its latest meal. A piece of downy feather blew off of the fox's bloody muzzle and flew off into the wind. The piece of goose down flew higher and higher in the wind currents until it was out of sight.

Chapter 6: What Comes Around

The cottonwood tree was growing quickly in the warm summer weather. It had a few small branches now, and a nice crown of leaves. As it swung slowly back and forth in the wind, a small piece of goose down floated past and stuck to the ever-rougher bark of the small tree. The down had traveled for miles on the wind, until it rested in this spot.

In the beaver pond, the industrious little engineers had created an even larger dam than they had the previous year. The result was that the pond expanded considerably.

Cottonwood
By Kevin J. Curtis

Several trees were now partially submerged; caught with their roots growing underwater. If this continued unchecked, they would slowly die.

The bottomland forest was dotted with areas of "ghost trees." These trees had grown to significant size, and then suffered a soggy death due to flooding. In the end, the trunks of these trees could stand for decades until the bark was worn off and most of the limbs were broken off by the wind. The result was an eerie "forest" of ghost trees.

The cottonwood was still safe, though the water had crept up near where it was growing. The soil around it remained moist, but not so wet that it would begin to rot. The beavers' projects were all around, and there was always the danger that one of the industrious little rodents would pick the cottonwood tree to chew down to eat its bark for food and then to use its trunk for construction of the dam or lodge.

So far the cottonwood had been overlooked, though many of the trees in the vicinity were either already cut down, or were in various states of being chewed down. In some cases, the size of some of the trees selected, caused the beavers to have to leave these projects and continue later. To a human, the ambitiousness of the little builders would seem almost absurd, as they sometimes worked for months on a single, over-sized tree.

There was a creek nearby that flowed into the beaver pond. This creek, where it was dammed, was the source of the water for the beaver pond. There was also a number of Brown Trout in the creek that attracted both humans and animals. With the seasonal flooding of the river, there was a large variety of fish in the deep beaver pond. The ambitious beavers had dredged the pond out to such a size and depth that would sustain it through a drought, even if the creek were to cease flowing. The beavers had succeeded in making a permanent change to

Cottonwood
By Kevin J. Curtis

the area, though the concept of "permanent" was a fragile one in a land that had been growing and changing for millions of years.

The last great ice age had carved the valley and bluffs, and the river continued to whittle the land as it sought to straighten the turns, and then to turn the straight sections of the riverbed. Eventually, humans would cause huge changes in this design as they used equipment to rearrange the landscape to their liking. But that would come later.

Along the bluff, two tiny figures could be seen walking down toward the creek. It was a young boy and girl. The two were siblings from a farm nearby, and each of them carried a cane pole and a basket. They intended to catch some of the trout in the stream. The girl was older, and she patiently showed her little brother how to bait the crude hook and toss the morsel into the creek. If nothing bit, they would pull it up and drop it again.

At first they weren't doing too well, but soon, by trial-and-error, they found the correct method to catch fish. After about an hour and a half, they had several trout in their baskets. That was when they noticed two tanned figures moving toward them.

The two American Indian boys were curious when they saw the other two children, and they decided to come closer. The two white children were slightly scared at first by the encounter, but they soon realized that the Indians were only curious. The girl showed the Indian boys how she used her cane pole to catch the fish. One Indian boy smiled and nodded, and then he reached for his bow and arrow. He aimed, and then shot into the water. The arrow missed. The other boy joined in, and after several attempts, one of them had finally hit a trout–and then dove into the creek to retrieve the fish.

The children were all laughing and having fun,

Cottonwood
By Kevin J. Curtis

though they did not know how to speak each other's language. Soon, the white children's father rode down from the bluff on his horse. As he approached, he shouted something to his son and daughter. He didn't seem to be too enthused about the children's new friendships. The boy and girl grabbed their baskets and cane poles and ran toward him.

The two Indian boys made ready to flee, but they soon realized that the man had only come to retrieve his children. When the man and his children were reunited, he turned his horse and the girl and boy followed behind him. Before they were out of sight, the little boy turned toward the two Indian boys and waved to them.

* * * *

As time passed, the cottonwood tree grew quickly. After a few years, it had a one-inch[5] diameter trunk. So far, the beavers had left this tree alone, and it continued to reach skyward.

There were many changes occurring in the bottomland forest. There were no longer any wolves living there. The continued campaign to eliminate Canis lupus, which was instituted by the white settlers, had succeeded. The wolves had been systematically shot, trapped and poisoned until there were no more. The elk were gone as well. Cougars were hunted too, though their solitary, nocturnal habits made them more difficult to eliminate–even though their numbers were significantly diminished.

The new human settlers also threatened many other animals. In addition, the growing numbers and influence of the European immigrants were displacing the indigenous people. The Native Americans were being systematically pushed off of their ancestral homelands. This was very difficult for them, as they held the spirits of their ancestors who were buried in this land in high regard. Some chose to

Copyright © 2008 by Kevin J. Curtis

Cottonwood
By Kevin J. Curtis

fight the whites, and though they were excellent warriors, they were unable to compete with the armaments of the white army.

One such group gathered one evening to ask for help from the Grandfathers who had passed before them. They had little food these days, but they scraped together as much as they could to have a feast to honor the spirits.

An elderly, yet powerful looking warrior wearing a wolf skin presided over the ceremony. There was a steady pulse of a drum, as he prepared a serving of food. This food, he held up to the four directions as he chanted to the steady heartbeat of the drum. The others watched silently… reverently as their spiritual leader continued, visible in the light of the fire they were gathered around. Then, the warrior set the food into the fire. The flames consumed the food, and the essence of it was given to the attending spirits in respect, and to satisfy their hunger.

Then the Chief came forward to address his people. They would leave this place when the Sun returned to the eastern sky from its sleep. They would find new hunting away from this place. The animals had gone from here, and the land now stunk from the animals that the white men kept. They could not be happy here any longer, and it was only a matter of time before they would be forced to move by the white army.

Some of the young men protested, but the leaders had made their decision. It was time to leave, and before they did, they would ask the spirits to guide them to a happier place.

* * * *

She was unsure of what was happening, but she knew that her father and mother were upset. In fact, everyone in the village seemed to be unraveled about something. She was only three-years-old, and this little

Cottonwood
By Kevin J. Curtis

Sioux girl sat wide-eyed, as the elders sat cross-legged in a circle. She was sitting on her grandfather's lap, as he spoke in a stern tone about things that she did not yet understand.

Outside of the circle, she watched as the women busily packed up all of the belongings. The men helped some, but most of the labor belonged to the women of the tribe. Her mother was busy and little Wachiwi, which translates into "Dancer," was content to sit on her grandfather's lap and stare at the flurry of activity around the encampment.

It was not unusual in American Indian culture, for a child to be present at an important council. Children were considered important, and no one thought it strange that Wahchinksapa, which translates into "Wise," would be discussing important matters while holding his young granddaughter.

In her childhood innocence, Wachiwi may have wondered what all of the fuss was about, even if she had understood that the conversation and packing was about the "Wasichus," or the non-Indian people in their ancestral lands. From her unique perspective, she may have thought that there was plenty of land and the white children might become her friends. In the reality of the world, she was on the fringe of an ideological battle between two cultures and two very different ways of life.

How could this child understand the frustration of her grandfather, as he tried to balance the need to protect his heritage, with the danger of fighting a war with the white army? Theirs was an unenviable position, as they were discussing the future of their children, and their children's children. How could little Wachiwi know that it was her future that hung in the balance?

She tugged playfully at her grandfather's necklace of bear teeth. She looked up at his kind face with her big brown eyes and smiled. Wahchinksapa smoothed the

Cottonwood
By Kevin J. Curtis

child's hair with a big beefy hand, and then readjusted her weight on his lap as he continued to speak. He told of how his heart was worried for the children of the tribe now that the Wasichus were fencing off the traditional hunting grounds of "the people."

Chapter 7: Cast of Characters

    Silas ground coffee beans for his evening coffee. He used a wooden bowl and the blunt end of a stick, just as his Ojibwe friend *Manidoo Makwa,* which translated, means "Spirit Bear," had used when he needed to grind something. Spirit Bear was gone now. He'd left with his people when they decided to flee from the whites.

    Silas was white, though he often appeared more like an American Indian. He dressed like the natives, and lived more like an Indian than a white man. Spirit Bear was his best friend, and Silas missed his company. Sitting alone in his shack, Silas felt the weight of loneliness as it crept inside. It seemed everyone he had ever known was gone.

    Of course, the other side of the story was that Silas had never been able to live the way most folks did. He hadn't the desire to be a farmer, and his hunter/trapper lifestyle didn't provide very well. It didn't make him good husband material either. He had been interested in his friend Spirit Bear's cousin, Prairie Flower, but her father had not approved of his daughter being with the white trapper.

    The girl Prairie Flower was gone now too. She had also left with her people. More than once, Silas wished he had followed the tribe. But even though he was a friend in good standing with Spirit Bear, he was not an Indian and the tribe had made the decision to leave the area inhabited by the whites. He was not welcome.

    He touched the bear-claw necklace that hung from

Cottonwood
By Kevin J. Curtis

his neck. It was a prized possession of Spirit Bear, and the Indian had given it to his friend as a gesture of friendship before he left. Spirit Bear had killed the bear as part of his initiation into manhood.

    Silas had given his friend the pistol that he had carried for the last decade. Silas had won the gun in a card game at the trading post. It had proven useful, as protection since then, but such a prize was just the thing to be given to his best friend when he was departing, possibly forever.

    He didn't have a percolator, and Silas stirred the ground coffee into a large mug that he filled with hot water from the pot on top of his wood stove. The liquid turned dark as he stirred. He let the mug sit on the edge of the stove to let the coffee grounds settle. He would drink most of it, but he customarily tossed out the bottom of the mug because of the grounds. When times were hard, and they almost always were, he would save the grounds to make a second or even third cup.

    He sat down in the chair he'd hewn from a log, and took a sip of the hot brew. It was strong and hot. The way he figured, there was nothing quite as satisfying as a mug of coffee made with fresh grounds–except for maybe a jug of whiskey or a beer and some company to share it with. Right now, he decided that he was lucky to have the coffee.

    Outside, it was getting dark. There were only two small windows in the shack, and the light outside was fading fast. There was a slight glow at the door of the wood stove, but Silas rarely stayed up very late into the night. The coffee would keep him awake for awhile, but since he'd never learned to read, there wasn't much to do at night.

    There was one thing that he did have, but he still hadn't mastered it. He opened a case, and took out an old fiddle. The violin was worn. Silas had gotten it after his uncle died many years ago. His uncle had been a fine fiddle

Cottonwood
By Kevin J. Curtis

player, and as a boy, Silas loved to hear him play. Uncle Dick had played many a party, wedding and wingding in his day, but he had died at an early age.

Silas had been pretty young at the time, but now he recollected that his uncle had been drunk most of the time–which may have contributed to his early demise. Alcoholism was common at the time, and those who drank too much, were often thought to have a lack of moral character. It wasn't until much later in history that alcoholism was classified as an addiction and treated as a disease.

Had he the resources, Silas may have ended up the same way. He liked his liquor well enough; he just couldn't usually afford it. He didn't have a still or grow corn, and others didn't part with their booze cheaply.

He plucked the strings, and attempted to tune the fiddle as best as he could. He wasn't tone deaf; he just wasn't exactly sure what he was doing. Uncle Dick had showed him a few things when he was a boy, but between the fact that it was a long time ago, and his uncle was most likely drunk at the time, he hadn't learned to play very well.

The violin made a sorrowful sound that matched Silas' mood. He played for an hour or so, until his fingers started to hurt from holding down the strings. The coffee was long gone by this time, and there was scarcely any light left, except the tiny glow from the door of the wood stove.

Silas placed the violin and bow back into the case and closed it up. He poured the coffee grounds onto a rag, so he could use them again tomorrow. His bed was short by modern standards, since people generally sat up as they slept. It was thought to be better for breathing that way.

The bed was little more than a crude frame with a rope tied across it to support his weight. On top of the rope

Cottonwood
By Kevin J. Curtis

was a layer of straw. Silas kicked off his well-worn boots, climbed into the bed and pulled a filthy old blanket over himself.

Outside in the distance, he could hear a coyote howl. He lay there listening for awhile, until he drifted off to sleep. Alone in his shack, Silas dreamt about playing his fiddle at a party, just as his uncle Dick had done long ago.

* * * *

He was a young Dakota Warrior. He had his own pony and possessed a man's bow, though he was by all accounts, still a young man. He had proven himself worthy of the honor of joining his elders in the sweat lodge. In preparation, he had not eaten for a day and night, and he sat in the lodge with the other men, to purify himself and to become closer to *Wakan Tanka,* who was the Creator of all things.

The men had stripped off their clothing, and sat cross-legged on the floor of the sweat lodge. The smoke of the prayer pipe mixed with the hot steam that came from water poured over a designated number of hot rocks.

The lodge had been constructed carefully, according to tradition. It was smudged to cleanse the area and the frame was made of willow branches. The sweat would last three or four hours, and was both a cleansing for the body, and a spiritual event to reduce ignorance and impurities of the soul.

The young man had recently been given the name, "Ohitekah," which meant "brave." He received this name after completing a *vision quest,* and returning from the wilderness with the skin of a huge Black Bear. These days, Ohitekah was consumed with the desire to win the heart of a certain Dakota girl, and he hoped to impress her with his deeds and growing status.

Cottonwood
By Kevin J. Curtis

The sweat lodge was dark with the doorway pulled shut, and the men sang songs, accompanied by the sound of drums. Ohitekah participated with much enthusiasm, as he was caught up in the singing and the stinging heat of the steam. The rhythms of the music pounded through his body and into the core of his existence. This was a "journey" that was his birthright, and something that he could share in, as his grandfathers did before him.

The intensity of the singing varied over the next few hours, and Ohitekah felt at times as if he was leaving his body and floating on the rhythmic sounds of the drums. He closed his eyes in the dark shelter. Beneath the coverings of animal hides, there was little light, except for the hot, glowing coals that heated the rocks.

Eventually, he reached a state of exhaustion and lightheadedness. He thought of the feast that would follow the sweat, and a new strength suddenly coursed through his body. The intensity of the music had reached a climax, and suddenly the men fell silent. Ohitekah opened his eyes, and he saw small lights, dancing around him and the other men. It was not a frightening vision, though it was unusual for the young man.

The lights continued to move effortlessly and quickly around the participants sitting in the sweat lodge. Ohitekah wondered if the others could see them as he did. That was when the spiritual leader announced that, "the spirits of our grandfathers are here with us now."

* * * *

Pierre had wandered these bluffs and this valley for a lifetime. He was 56 years old by now–at least as much as he could recollect. He moved slowly along an old trail, encumbered by the weight of the pack that was strapped to his back. He stopped momentarily, to poke a stubby finger at the tooth that was decayed and infected in his mouth. He

Cottonwood
By Kevin J. Curtis

tasted blood, and spat. He reckoned his old body had seen better days. Now he was paying the price for being old and living hard.

Pierre had been born to an American Indian mother and a French fur-trapper father. He remembered little of his childhood except that he once had a sister and as far as he knew, she lived somewhere in the city. Pierre couldn't stand the city and was only at home out here in the wilderness.

Actually, he had never felt at home anywhere else. One thing that resonated throughout his entire existence was that he was different. Sure there were others like him, half-breeds, who were not quite Indian and not quite white.

Suddenly a childhood memory flashed through his mind. The other children at the one-room schoolhouse where he briefly attended as a boy were taunting him. The fight had been brutal and the numbers lopsided–and he had taken a beating from several other children. Worst of all, there was a girl who was older than he was, who had finished him off with a right cross to the jaw. It was "lights out," and he never returned to school after he finally regained his senses.

Why had he remembered that he wondered? He continued on along the trail. With each step, he could feel the continuous pain in his left knee. It was as if someone was trying to pry off his kneecap with a knife. He began to limp a little.

As his mind continued to wander, Pierre remembered that winter about six years ago. He was crossing the marsh just west of here, when the ice broke beneath his feet. He sprawled out on his stomach to spread out his weight, but he was carrying a heavy pack and he soon found himself wallowing in the muddy water beneath the ice.

Cottonwood
By Kevin J. Curtis

The cold water took his breath away, and he was fortunate that it wasn't deep where he was. Still, he fought hard against the sinking mud and the cold that made his entire body shudder. When he finally got out, he needed to get warm and dry or he wouldn't survive. Somehow, probably something his father had taught him… Pierre had worked blindly with frozen hands until he managed to get a spark burning on a dry bird's nest. He had gotten a lifesaving fire started and had managed to stave off death for another day.

Pierre shuddered involuntarily. He felt a chill, though his hike had caused him to workup a sweat. He poked once again at the loose and bloody tooth in his mouth. As he continued his journey, he remembered the time he had found a frozen corpse in these woods. The man looked ghost-like, as his entire body was frozen solid. Pierre recalled going through the dead man's belongings. It was midwinter, and whatever the dead couldn't use was fair game for the living as far as he was concerned.

He turned to climb up the bank, out of the river valley. The ravine was unremarkable, considering that Pierre had traversed hundreds just like it in his lifetime. But the tired old body of the trapper was not as resilient as it had once been. He struggled with his burden against gravity and the wet, slippery leaves beneath his feet.

Suddenly a pain shot through his chest and arm, just as he felt his body start to fall. It was surreal, and he seemed to have sufficient time to notice himself airborne before he landed on the hard ground. There was a sharp branch beneath him, and he struggled as the pain shot through his back. He managed to free himself from the discomfort underneath him, but he found that he was unable to move his right arm or leg. He struggled briefly, but the weight of the pack was still secured firmly to his back.

Cottonwood
By Kevin J. Curtis

Pierre lay where he was, unable to move and completely exhausted. His mind kept racing through what he must do to survive, but his body would not cooperate. Finally, he lay there, going in and out of consciousness. There was no one to help him. His solitary existence was doomed to a slow death halfway up that ravine.

He lay alone as the darkness set in. He was afraid that a cougar or a bear might come along and find him in this helpless state. Finally, he decided that there was nothing more he could do. At this point, Pierre was finally able to die. His body lay on that lonely spot. His eyes were open, reflecting the dim moonlight that filtered down through the trees.

* * * *

Nearly two years later, Michelle Dubois heard a knock at her door, in the bustling mill town of Minneapolis. It was a telegram from her aunt across the river in St. Paul. Someone had found the skeletal remains of a body. It was thought to be Pierre… her brother. Not much else was found except for an old rifle and a knife that another trapper identified as belonging to Pierre.

Michelle had not seen her older brother for over a decade. He had been unaccustomed to even the most basic "necessities" of civilized life. Whenever she had seen him after their childhood, Michelle could hardly stand his rank smell and crude habits. Eventually, she moved to the city with her husband–who worked in the mill. She had more or less successfully thrown off the "half-breed" stigma, and had been absorbed into white civilization.

"Pierre," she whispered. Her mind fluttered back to her childhood. Her legs felt weak, and she found her rocking chair and sat down.

* * * *

Copyright © 2008 by Kevin J. Curtis

Cottonwood
By Kevin J. Curtis

As the cottonwood continued to grow, many changes and many happenings occurred nearby. Life and death continued amidst the changes to the land and the human and animal populations within and surrounding the bottomland forest.

With the displacement of the Native Americans, farming continued to grow in the area. This use of the land, forced many animals to either adapt to man, or perish. Most of the wild animals were adversely affected by the new humans. The new human population brought with them domesticated animals that competed for grazing. They brought dogs that they used in hunting, especially for the large carnivores. Even their domestic cats sometimes had litters that went feral and preyed upon songbirds, instead of the mice and rats that they were intended to control. Many of these same varieties of mice and rats were just some of the many exotic species of plants and animals that were introduced either intentionally, or by accident by the new human population.

One species of bird that was introduced was the pheasant. These game birds were originally from Asia, but they adapted well to the meadows and new farm fields. They were soon to become an important game bird for hunters.

There were also some animals introduced that overpopulated and drove out the indigenous species. One such species was the European Carp. These resilient fish were brought by the white settlers as a potential food source. They soon began to displace the native species and overpopulate ponds, lakes and rivers.

This was not a widely understood concept at the time. Conservation was not practiced in those early days. It wasn't until later that people realized that damaging the land or wildlife might reduce the quality of life for the human inhabitants as well.

Cottonwood
By Kevin J. Curtis

Throughout all of this, the cottonwood tree continued to grow taller and wider. Each ring of growth held a piece of the history of its world inside of it. At the very center, the core was reddish, as was the blood of the warrior who bled on the tree in its infancy. Later, after a few decades, this core would be largely replaced by a hollow space. The cottonwoods tended to hollow out as they aged, which provided excellent shelter for a variety of wildlife. These huge trees were truly magnificent in both their enormity and the diversity of life that used them for living spaces.

One particularly pleasant summer's day, a man walked along the bluff with his son. They were heading down to the river to fish. In those days, the river was still clean and even if it wasn't, no one yet knew about the harmfulness of industrial toxins that would later cause so much devastation and contaminate the water and the fish in it.

The man moved down the hill slowly. His son was up ahead of him, but the boy stopped frequently to look back for his father. The man was a farmer, and he had recently suffered a life-changing accident. The stump that remained where his left arm was supposed to be, gave a hint as to the extent of the damage incurred by the machinery he had been caught in.

The corn shredder was powered by a long belt, connected to the power drive of a tractor. This was state-of-the-art farming equipment (at the time), and it was designed to remove the cobs of corn from the stalk. The "business end" of the machine definitely had some very sharp moving parts, and a clog had prompted the farmer to put his hand too far into the machine to try to free it up.

The man had been helping on his neighbor's farm, as was customary in those days. Some jobs were too difficult to accomplish alone, and often farmers would pool

Cottonwood
By Kevin J. Curtis

their resources and talent and work on large projects, one farm at a time. It so happened that this man was helping his neighbor when the unfortunate accident occurred.

It should be noted at this time in the history of the United States, that there were none of the lawsuits, liabilities and insurance claims associated with what would take place later. It was generally believed that accidents, however unfortunate or debilitating that they may be, were bound to happen. Only God could know why such things happened.

This was also a time when the art of medicine had many more limitations than it would have later. Such an injury was indeed, potentially life-threatening. Not only could the injury itself be deadly, but the risk of infection was also a huge factor in the survival of the victim.

The man made it to the edge of the river, where he watched his son bait his crude fishhook and begin to fish. He looked at the end of the stub of arm he still had, and saw the dark stain where the wound still seeped blood. It had been three weeks since the machine had caught hold of his shirt sleeve and pulled his hand into it.

His fingers were nearly pulled off, and the lower arm and the hand had been crushed and mutilated. When he was finally brought to the care of the local doctor, he had lost a lot of blood and was in shock. The doctor managed to save the farmer's life, but not before he was forced to amputate the limb above the crushed and mangled portion. A week later, the gangrene had set-in, and the doctor had been forced to remove all but the smallest amount of the man's arm below the shoulder.

The farmer filled his cheek with tobacco, and then spat onto the ground. His neighbors had been helping with his farm and the chores, but they had too much to do on their own to continue this forever. He looked at his son fishing at the water's edge. The boy had been working so

Cottonwood
By Kevin J. Curtis

hard that his father began to worry about him. He had already left the school to help on the farm. It was a lot to ask of a boy his age.

The farmer spat again. He had tried to talk his son into going fishing, but the boy had refused until his father said that he wanted to go with him. Finally, the boy agreed, and he was now enjoying himself at the river's edge, still looking back occasionally–protective of his father. The boy had, at least momentarily, recaptured his boyhood as he pulled in a large pike.

His father nodded approvingly as the boy showed off his catch. He had been forced to grow up too quickly since his father's accident. The farmer spat again and hung his head. After a few minutes, he looked up. His son was smiling, and ready to go home with his catch. That was when the farmer decided that he would be strong for his children. His family needed him to pull out of his depression. For them, he would continue on.

As they walked across the edge of the marsh toward home, the farmer spat tobacco juice and it landed next to the cottonwood tree. As the father and son continued up the bluff, the tobacco soaked into the soil.

Later that evening, as the sun began to go down below the bluffs, a large form came ambling along the edge of the marsh. It lifted its large head and sniffed the air. To a sensitive ear, the sound of the bear's puffing could be heard. This was an old animal that had been around for a number of years. As the old bear aged, he found it more difficult to find adequate food. As white settlers kept building their farms within the river valley, their garbage, livestock and crops became an easy source of food for this aged bruin to use to fatten himself before his winter hibernation.

The bear's eyes were not particularly good, but his nose was very acute. He stopped near the cottonwood tree

Cottonwood
By Kevin J. Curtis

and smelled hard. He found the tobacco that the farmer had spit out. The old bear first took his nose and rooted in the soil. Then his tongue came out and he licked up the tobacco soaked spot.

Bears were not fussy, and being true omnivores, they did not turn much down if it had any kind of an odor that they found intriguing. Such items might include soap, leather, garbage or whatever they could find.

This trait, in an older animal, particularly one that was gaining interest in human possessions, was bound to lead to disastrous ends. As the chill of fall became noticeable, both man and animals were making ready for the oncoming winter. The farmers were working the harvest and the women were canning fruits and vegetables and curing meat. The wild animals of the bottomland forest were either storing away supplies of food like the squirrels and mice, or they were eating as much as possible before the snow and cold came, like the bears.

The old bear was finished with the tobacco soaked soil, and he wanted something more substantial. This led him to a nearby farm. This bear had visited farms previously, so he was accustomed to the proximity of humans and their animals. In fact, this bear had developed a taste for garbage and for chickens in this way. He had also tasted the produce from the vegetable garden and the only reason he didn't spend more time at the farm, was because of the farm dogs.

The bear wasn't particularly afraid of the dogs, though they were of good size. The bear was more than a match for the pair of them. It was more a matter of the constant noise that the dogs were able to create that the bear found so distasteful. The two dogs could bark and howl like crazy! The dogs were also very quick. They could run in, harass the bear and run away before it could swing its deadly paw and strike them down.

Cottonwood
By Kevin J. Curtis

This bear had killed a dog once. It had been about a year ago when a man was using "bear hounds" to hunt bears. These hounds were trained to track and find bears for the bear hunter. The hound had been sent with two others like him after the bear. When they caught up to it, the hounds were so crazed with the hunt that they attacked the bear. One of the dogs got too close and the bear lashed out with a wicked paw. The claws caught hold of the dog's head and nearly tore it off. The two remaining hounds continued the battle briefly, before they were chased off with wounds of their own. The bear had made his escape just before the hunters arrived.

On this particular evening, the bear had managed to make his way onto the farm without the dogs noticing. This was because the dogs had followed the farmer off into the field, where he was hoping to find a bird or rabbit to shoot for some table meat.

The bear smelled something good, and he headed directly toward that smell. This brought him to the door of the log cabin that the farm family lived in. Inside, mother and daughter were busily preparing the evening meal. The smell of the food cooking was too much for the bear to resist, and he was soon standing inside of the door, looking at the surprised women inside. The mother grabbed a pan and after banging it against the stove, she threw it at the uninvited guest. The girl followed suit, and they began a noisy barrage of throwing things at the bear. The interloper stopped, and was suddenly a little bit unsure of his situation. A cast iron pot hit the bear in the head, and made him back out of the door. He shook off the blow, and as he started back in, the two women threw the door shut and dropped the board that served as a lock into place.

This stopped the bear briefly, but he was also getting annoyed. This animal was growing more aggressive and more desperate due to his advanced age. He tried

Cottonwood
By Kevin J. Curtis

pushing on the door and it creaked beneath his weight as he leaned on it. The women began to scream, and that was when the two dogs arrived on the scene.

These farm dogs, while brave enough, weren't willing to get too close to the huge bear that had trespassed onto their farm. They worked together, one on each side, nipping at the large beast and then turning to run when it would wield back on them. The two together, were able to keep the bear frustrated and still stay out of its reach.

The three animals growled and turned around on each other. Thankfully for the women in the cabin, they moved away from the door and into the yard. The noise became intense as the dogs kept up a continuous barrage of barking and howling. The actual damage inflicted in the fight was minimal–since the dogs employed their "hit-and-run" tactics and the bear was unable to connect with his swift attackers.

Finally, the bear had enough and he began to run, with the two dogs in pursuit. He stopped halfway across the yard and turned once again on the dogs, but the canines swiftly dodged the attack. That was when a crack echoed across the farmyard. The bear stopped cold, and turned toward the sound. The smoke was still coming out of the shotgun when another gunshot rang out from the side. The farmer had heard the ruckus and came from the field with his shotgun already loaded from his hunting. His son, who never seemed to be far from his rifle also heard the noise and fired a few seconds later.

The bear roared in pain, and dropped to the ground. Almost immediately, he jumped back up and went after the dogs, which were still in close proximity. This time there were simultaneous gunshots and again the bear dropped to the ground, still struggling. The two men reloaded and shot a third round into the wounded black bear. Then… suddenly there was quiet.

Cottonwood
By Kevin J. Curtis

Chapter 8: What Floated In

As the cold set in, William was released from his job working on the riverboat. The river was starting to ice up, and there would be no river traffic until after the spring melt. He sat in the back of the wagon and pulled his jacket tighter around himself. The wind was cold today and he was anxious to get home and have some of his mother's cooking. He was also hoping to see his neighbors' daughter Annie, who lived on the next farm.

The two had met as children, and had become closer as the years went by. At age 17, William had decided to leave the farm and go to work as a deckhand on the barges that carried goods and supplies up and down the Minnesota and sometimes the Mississippi river. It paid pretty well, so his pa couldn't argue with his son's choice to leave the farm.

William and his pa never seen eye-to-eye on things anyway. In those days, life was hard and many of these men ruled their families with a very heavy hand. To oppose the will of his father when he was a child was an act that he would regret. His father used an oak branch or a leather belt to whip his children into submission. The strain on their relationship was hard for the boy. Mostly because after he left the farm, he missed his ma and his brother and sister. Above all, he missed Annie.

The wagon he rode in belonged to Annie's father, and William had hitched a ride with Mr. Fretheim and his son, who owned a farm near William's parents' farm. William would spend the winter with his parents and siblings, unless he and his father couldn't get along. He wasn't sure what he would do then. He decided to deal with that if and when it happened. Right now, all he could think about was Annie.

Cottonwood
By Kevin J. Curtis

The wagon pulled into the Fretheim farm and stopped near the barn. Annie saw it coming, threw on her coat, and tried to look as dignified as she could while nearly running out the door to meet it. In the back, behind her father and brother, was her William! She could barely contain herself, though she had to maintain control while her father and brother were still present.

She greeted her father and brother and then turned to William who was standing behind them. She said, "Hello William," in a calm tone. He smiled at her, and noticed the tear running down her cheek. Mr. Fretheim and his son decided to head straight into the barn. They could unhitch the horse in a few minutes.

With the Fretheim men safely out of sight, Annie threw herself into William's arms, and he held her there until the chill of the biting wind forced them to go inside where Mrs. Fretheim was already pouring the coffee.

William had many stories to tell and the Fretheim children were mesmerized by the tales. William sipped his coffee and told about the body that had floated up one day. It was so badly decomposed that it was hard to identify. William had helped to recover the bloated corpse. No one was sure who it was, but it was thought to possibly be that of a farmer who had disappeared not far from here.

The children squirmed as they sat on the outskirts of the kitchen where the guest was talking. Soon, much too soon for Annie, William announced that he had better get home before it got any later. He wished them all a goodbye, winked at Annie, thanked Mr. Fretheim for the ride back and was out the door.

The hike home was only about a mile, but it was cold, getting dark and William had his possessions slung over his back. He had a sense of foreboding about seeing his pa, but he could already taste his ma's cooking and he missed his brother and sister. Maybe things would be better

Cottonwood
By Kevin J. Curtis

this time he thought. After all, his brother Roger, and sister Catherine didn't have much trouble with their pa. William was always the adventurous type and trouble always seemed to find his antics.

Roger didn't test his father's patience like William did. He was a steady farmhand and knew when to be quiet. Though he was two years younger than William was, he was already bigger than his father and showed no signs that he was done growing. This may have also helped his situation with his pa.

Catherine was the youngest, though she was mature for her years. She was the mirror image of her mother in many ways and at age 13, she was already a good cook and proficient at canning, curing and all the domestic chores. She doted on her father both out of respect and fear, and was seldom the recipient of any harsh words.

He was still about a quarter of a mile from the farmhouse when two forms ran out of the woods and surrounded him. The barking dogs sounded alarmed and aggressive as they positioned themselves on each side of William.

"Hey guys!" William said.

Instantly the tone of the two animals' voices changed and they began wagging their tails and moved in close. It was the two farm dogs, and they recognized William though they hadn't seen him since last spring. They jumped up on William and tried to lick his face. He pushed them down and one grabbed the bottom of his pant leg and gave it a tug.

"Okay… stay down now!" he commanded.

The dogs settled a bit though they were still extremely excited to see William and they jumped up and down as he talked to them. With the two dogs in the lead, William walked through the gate and back into the world of his childhood. He was home.

Cottonwood
By Kevin J. Curtis

As William walked up the farmyard in the dim moonlight, he was surprised to find a huge, dark form hanging in the cherry tree near the log house. When he got closer, he saw that it was a huge bearskin that was hung in the tree to dry.

"I didn't know anyone here was a bear hunter," he said aloud to himself. He knocked twice on the door and then lifted the latch and went in.

Once inside, his ma ran up and hugged her son. Then Catherine gave her big brother a hug. Roger extended his beefy hand to his brother, and finally, William's pa, who was sitting at the table, said,

"Welcome home son. You're just in time for your ma's chicken and dumplings."

William smiled. He pulled up a chair near his father and sat down. His ma ladled some food onto a plate and set it before him. His little sister put some silverware down next to it.

The family settled back down around the table. The stove was warm and the lantern gave off a cheery glow as the family was reunited. William took a mouthful of the chicken and dumplings and it was as good as he had remembered it was. Nowhere had he found a meal better than his ma could make.

"How'd your season on the river go Will?" asked Roger.

"It was good. There's a lot to tell," started William. "But first, one of you has to tell me about that bearskin hangin' in the cherry tree!"

The family erupted into laughter, and the night closed in around the cabin. Inside it was warm and friendly. Outside the two farm dogs curled up together in front of the door and all was well.

* * * * *

Copyright © 2008 by Kevin J. Curtis

Cottonwood
By Kevin J. Curtis

Winter arrived once again to the Minnesota River Valley. In the bottomland forest, the cottonwood tree was in dormancy for the winter. It had grown significantly during each summer of its existence. It was on its way to becoming one of the huge trees of the river valley. But that would still take some time. While cottonwoods are fast growing, to reach the height and girth of the giants of its kind would take many more years.

William and Roger were hunting deer and the two brothers passed very near to the cottonwood. They decided to sit in one of the trees near where the cottonwood was growing. They picked a sturdy looking tree and climbed up, high enough where they could be above and out of sight of any White-tailed deer that might come by. There were deer in the area from time to time, but they were also very alert and hard to get close to. At this point in history, there were fewer deer due to hunting and lack of game management. Years later, White-tailed deer would overpopulate some areas due to the lack of natural predators.

The two men were dressed in layers, including long underwear, warm coats and boots. William had a wool cap and Roger's was made of a warm rabbit fur. Each of them had a hot baked potato inside of their pockets to keep their hands warm. The potato was also a good snack if they were out for a long time. They positioned themselves in the tree so that they were facing opposite directions. This way they could communicate quietly and keep watch for deer from all directions.

Winter, especially early on, was a good time for the brothers to go hunting. The cold weather meant that there was less to do on the farm and they could always use extra meat. After nearly an hour, a small buck broke out of the cover of the brush near the marsh. William saw it from his position and he motioned Roger to stay quiet as he took

Cottonwood
By Kevin J. Curtis

aim. His gun rang out and the buck jumped forward for a short distance before he fell into the snow near a thicket.

The brothers climbed down quickly and ran to where the deer had fallen. William's aim was good, and further examination showed that his bullet had pierced the animal's heart. The brothers pulled the deer out of the thicket and it lay very near to the cottonwood tree as they gutted it and prepared to bring it back to the farm.

When they were done, the snow was painted crimson red and the gut pile lay close to the cottonwood tree. Inside the stomach were the partially digested remains of the leaves, grass and twigs the animal had been feeding on. Over the next few days, many animals would visit the remains. Eventually, some of the leftover deer would seep into the soil that the cottonwood was growing in.

William and Roger tied a rope onto the buck and they each grabbed an end and they began to drag the deer through the snow toward home. It was less than a mile back, but the two brothers were tired by the time they reached the barn. They hung the gutted deer from the rafters of the barn and went inside to warm up and quench their thirst.

They had scarcely noticed on the way home, but the sky had grown dark and snow was falling. By the time they left the barn to go into the log house, the snow had started falling hard. William knew that Annie was safe at home on the neighboring farm, but with no telephones (or electricity) there was no way to know for sure.

Meanwhile at the Fretheim house, Annie was thinking about William, and hoping that he and Roger had come back from hunting by now. She looked out of the window and saw the snow starting to pile up. She could barely see the barn now and the snow was coming down harder.

Cottonwood
By Kevin J. Curtis

  Her father came in from outside with a long coil of hempen rope in his gloved hand. He had tied the other end to the barn, so that if the blizzard got really bad and visibility was little or none, he could still find his way between the house and the barn by using the rope. Annie began to wonder if there was a rope long enough to reach William's house. Suddenly she realized that a tear was running down her cheek. She wiped her face and tried to appear cheerful.
  "Things is gettin' bad out der now," said Mr. Fretheim. "It's a good thing 'dem boys on the next farm got back when they did."
  "You saw William?" asked Annie.
  "Yah," started Mr. Fretheim. "Him and Roger got 'demselves a deer they were pullin' back. I reckon they made it back jus' in time."
  Annie turned back toward the window again. Another tear had escaped from the other eye now, only this time it wasn't because she was worried. Now that she knew William was safe, the snow outside looked a lot prettier. She stared through the window as the snow piled up outside.
  That night the wind howled and the snow fell heavy. William Schmidt lay in the loft above the kitchen, listening to the wind howl. His brother Roger snored softly nearby. Privacy was a luxury that the Schmidt family couldn't afford right now. They had talked about expanding the house again.
  Originally, the log cabin had one room that served all functions. As the family grew, the loft was added for a place for the children to sleep, and a new "wing" was added to one side so Mr. and Mrs. Schmidt had some privacy. Catherine had a nook in the corner with a curtain that she could pull for privacy.

Cottonwood
By Kevin J. Curtis

In the loft, William and Roger actually had plenty of room horizontally, but the vertical space was restricted by the slanted pitch of the roof. Even in the center where it was highest, William could only kneel. There was a comfortable bed of straw to sleep on, and the vents from down below let up some heat from the kitchen. Still, it was necessary to wrap up in a warm blanket or a quilt to stay warm. The house was by nature, drafty and the wood stove seemed to be either too hot or not hot enough.

William mused at the irony of his situation. All summer as he worked as a deckhand on the river, he thought about how far away Annie was and he worried that she might not miss him. Now, he knew that she had missed him, but even though she was a short hike away, the weather had intervened and a blizzard now separated them as sure as if there was still a hundred miles between them.

Chapter 9: Water, Earth, Sky and the Passage of Time

The Johnson's moved to Minnesota by way of Alabama. They were hoping to avoid racial discrimination by moving up north, but in 1941, there was still plenty of it to go around. The family moved onto a plot of land that they could afford, after securing a loan that would keep them in debt for a long time. They intended to farm the land that they bought, though it was less-than-desirable, due to frequent flooding after the spring snow melt, or after heavy rains.

Known by their neighbors as "the blacks," the Johnson family settled in, raising a few farm animals and some vegetables and crops. They were primarily subsistence farmers, and they would trade any surplus to acquire those things that they could not produce on the family farm.

Cottonwood
By Kevin J. Curtis

Shortly after moving in and beginning to work the farm, they found out about the seriousness of the flood situation. They grabbed whatever they could carry and headed for higher ground. Before the water rose up over the farm, Lester Johnson let the animals free of their pens and cages. He decided it was better to risk losing them by letting them free, than it was to find them drowned when the floodwaters receded.

Their neighbors did not welcome the family when they turned up homeless from the flooding. After spending nearly a week living at the edge of the woods, the water finally receded enough for them to return to the farm. All of the buildings were damaged or destroyed. Many of the animals never returned and the crops were ruined. Eventually, the Johnson's had little choice but to leave the farm.

Now, burdened with a mortgage for land that they could not farm, or subsequently afford, they defaulted on their loan and the bank foreclosed on the land they had purchased. Eventually, the family moved to St. Paul, where they found employment in the service industry. Theirs was not a happy ending, though they had at least found work.

* * * *

The blacks had moved away, and Jimmy and Marcus were exploring the land where their farm had been. It was in bad repair from the continued flooding, but the boys were using what was left of the house for a "fort."

The boys were so busy playing, that they scarcely noticed that the sky had become prematurely dark. When they finally heard that first crack of thunder, they both looked out of the door of the house, stunned by the dark greenish color of the sky.

"It's going to storm!" Jimmy shouted.

Cottonwood
By Kevin J. Curtis

    Without delay, the two boys ran from the house and headed up the ridge toward home. They had been through a number of storms in the river valley, and they had witnessed the aftermath of destruction from floods, hail and high winds.

    The wind began to howl when the boys reached the top of the ridge. Off to the north, they could see a black wall of clouds moving quickly toward them like a train. They felt the coolness of the air, and they knew that they had only moments until the storm would be on top of them.

    They looked toward the root cellar, and saw their mother at the entrance shouting something that was carried off by the howling wind. Just then, their father rushed up behind them and grabbed both boys, one in each arm, and ran to the cellar entrance. He handed the boys down to their mother, and he and the family dog tumbled in behind, just as the rain and hail started falling.

    Inside of the root cellar, it was dark and damp. It was not a place where one would want to spend much time. At the moment, however, it was the best place that any of them could be. Outside, the storm grew in fury, as the wind increased and the lightning and thunder began shaking the ground and lighting up the valley.

    Huddled together in the cellar, Jimmy could smell sweat and also the wet dog. These smells combined with the earthy odors of stored fruits and vegetables and the musty smell of mold and mildew. His little brother Marcus was wide-eyed, listening to the sounds above the trapdoor–sounds of what was going on in the upper world outside. The storm continued for what seemed to be a long time. The cramped, damp cellar developed the qualities of both being stuffy and chilly at the same time.

    When the noise above finally stopped, Buzz, the boys' father, cautiously opened the door and the family emerged into the darkness of night. As far as its light could

Cottonwood
By Kevin J. Curtis

reach, the lantern that they carried revealed the destruction left behind by the storm. The chicken coop was overturned. Buzz pulled on the door, and soggy chickens emerged. Further investigation found that several birds had suffocated beneath the bodies of the others.

The house was relatively intact, though part of the roof had been torn off by the strong winds. The section of roof lay broken on the ground some distance away. It was difficult to assess the full extent of damages in the dark, so the family walked toward the farmhouse door to seek shelter until morning. As they neared the doorway, the lantern cast a shadowy light toward the barn, where the outline of the old cottonwood tree was noticeable, lying on top of the crushed barn roof.

Just then, Marcus started wailing. He was upset and could barely speak. He had left his toy truck on the front steps earlier that day. All the while he was in the cellar, the little boy wondered if his favorite toy was still there. Now, he found it missing. The toy was made by his father, cut out of a branch of the cottonwood tree that now lay across the barn roof.

His mother brought him into the house and dried his eyes. She told him that they could find another toy truck for him, but the important thing was that the family, including the dog, "Dodger," was safe. She hugged him and told Marcus that they had been lucky to survive the storm and that was what really mattered.

Just then, Dodger came up and licked Marcus's face and made the boy laugh. He squirmed and his mom let him go and then he and Jimmy ran for the loft. When they climbed up, they could see outside where the roof had been torn off. Buzz climbed the ladder to the loft, and told the boys to sleep downstairs tonight. He said that they would fix the roof tomorrow.

Copyright © 2008 by Kevin J. Curtis

Cottonwood
By Kevin J. Curtis

"Get to sleep!" Buzz told his boys. "We have a lot of work to do tomorrow and we need to start early."

After all of the excitement, no one fell asleep right away. Eventually though, exhaustion took its toll, and the house was quiet.

* * * *

Much later, a considerable distance away, a boy was fishing in the Minnesota River. He noticed something in the mud near the shore where he was. The mud was thick and deep, and he knew that he needed to be careful or he would sink down and possibly fall into the swift current of the river.

Carefully, he used a long stick to dislodge the object from the mud and pull it closer onto the shore. It was covered in mud by the time the boy recovered the object, but it was unmistakably a toy truck. Wherever it had come from was a mystery, as was how it ended up in the river.

The boy scanned the shoreline, suddenly aware that there may have been a child holding the toy when it fell into the river. Seeing nothing out of the ordinary, he sat down on a log and began to clean the mud off of the toy truck. It was in remarkably good condition, despite having been fished out of the river.

The toy was made of wood, probably homemade. It was unremarkable, though unmistakably a truck in design. When the boy had cleaned enough mud off of it, he noticed that there was a word carved into the bottom of the toy truck. He cleaned that area, and discovered that it said, "Marcus."

The young fisherman didn't know anyone named Marcus, but he set the toy next to his fishing bucket. He would take it home and if no one else knew who Marcus was, he would give it to his little brother.

Cottonwood
By Kevin J. Curtis

* * * *

Many years later, in an antique store in Stillwater, Minnesota, a young family walked through, looking at the items for sale. They had two little boys, and the older one found the truck and was inspecting it.

"They made toys out of wood?" He asked.

"Yes they did," answered his father. "This old truck must be a hundred years old!"

The younger boy stared at the toy that his father and brother were looking at.

"Look!" said the older brother, "it has Marcus's name on it!"

Sure enough, the name Marcus was scratched into the bottom of the wooden truck.

"Hey!" said the father, showing the youngest boy, "it has your name on it!"

The little boy looked at the word. He was too young to read, but the lettering looked familiar to him, so he smiled and reached for the truck.

Later that evening, the family was back at home, and Marcus sat on the floor of the living room, pushing the truck across the carpet. He made sounds like an engine as he played. Suddenly he stopped. He turned the toy upside-down, and looked at the word carved underneath. "Marcus!" he said, pointing at it. His parents smiled, and marveled at how this simple wooden toy had become such a favorite amongst the plastic toys scattered about the house.

Chapter 10: Earthen Mounds

Spring had returned to the bottomland forest. The years had been kind to the cottonwood tree and it had a diameter of about a foot now.[6] More white people had settled in the surrounding area and their influence was far-

Cottonwood
By Kevin J. Curtis

reaching. As time went on, more of the things that these people used were discarded. Some of these things could be found on their farms, in their towns, in the rivers, lakes and in the surrounding woods and prairies. Littering was common, and it would take the human population a little while to catch-up with the negative effects of how and where they discarded unwanted things.

Because of this trend to dump unused materials, an old disc was rusting away near the marsh where the cottonwood tree was growing. The disc was once used to breakup soil clumps in farm fields. This one had been used with a horse team. It had been discarded when the farmer had purchased new equipment and new farming implements. The changes that began with the white settlers had not ceased, and actually seemed to increase as new technology developed. The land still held a history though, and some of it remained very powerful.

The slight, steady, regular sound of water came from the river on the morning breeze. There was fog, and drizzle fell as the canoe broke through the shroud of moist air and bumped the edge of the riverbank. A tall, thin man emerged from the canoe, stepped into the water, and then pulled his wooden canoe onto dry land. He wore very little clothing and his skin was dark brown and his long black hair hung down his back. He was American Indian, and he had come to this place for a specific reason.

He walked almost silently into the woods, keeping alert for signs of the whites. His people had occupied this land when he was a small boy, but they had left early one morning–the whole village, and they had never returned. Now Screaming Hawk (Weh Sah Gway Kaikaik) had returned after all of this time to visit the land of his dead ancestors.

His father was buried near here. Now that his mother had died, he had come back to visit his father's

Copyright © 2008 by Kevin J. Curtis

Cottonwood
By Kevin J. Curtis

spirit and ask him to welcome her back into the tribe that lived in the otherworld. Finding the exact location of his father's burial spot would be nearly impossible, since the Indians did not mark their graves.

Screaming Hawk walked past the cottonwood tree and started cautiously up the bluff. He knew the whites lived somewhere above, but he also knew the spot he sought was near the top. Then, he noticed it. Most men would have walked right past and not recognized where they were, but Screaming Hawk had found what he was looking for.

The tall Indian sat down on the ground and pulled a pouch from his waist. He opened it and removed a chamois that he unrolled on the ground. Inside, there was a stone pipe and a smaller pouch filled with tobacco and willow bark. He loaded the pipe and lit it. He sat motionless with his eyes closed, praying.

The sweet smoke from the prayer pipe filled his mouth, and then as he slowly blew it out, it carried his prayers on the wind up to the realm of the Creator. Underneath one of the mounds of earth that dotted the hillside around him, was the place where Screaming Hawk's father had been laid to rest.

It was unlikely after all these years that much if anything remained of his father's body. There was also no way to know which mound was his. None of this mattered to Screaming Hawk now, as he smoked his prayer pipe and continued to pray. The place of the dead was still very powerful, and he had not eaten or drank since he left his village two days ago. He was on a *vision quest,* and it wasn't long before he noticed a man walking near to him.

With his eyes open now, Screaming Hawk watched as the man emerged from the shroud of fog and approached him. The apparition nodded at the warrior, who still held the smoldering stone pipe. Then the ghost from the past

Cottonwood
By Kevin J. Curtis

walked right through his son and over to a barely discernable mound nearby, where he sat cross-legged facing his living son. Slowly, Screaming Hawk repositioned himself so that he was facing the spirit of his father.

"This one is mine," said the father to his son. "I was buried here many years ago when you were still a boy."

"I remember," said Screaming Hawk.

"These are the others, who are here with me," said his father, as he motioned with his arm across the landscape of mounds. One by one, the rest of the dead came into view and made themselves known.

"I am honored," replied Screaming Hawk. "I have come here for wisdom to bring to my people. I have come to ask for direction, and I have come to honor my ancestors."

"The world is a very different place now my son," began the spirit. "No longer do our people live in these bluffs along this river. They have all left here or they have died or become absorbed by the whites. I know of the reservations, and the poverty. Things will be bad. They will be bad for your whole life my son. It will be against the white mans' laws to go on vision quest and to practice our ways. One day though, the grandchildren of these people will feel ashamed. Then, finally, the government will see the errors that they have made and they will allow our language, our prayers and our spirituality to exist openly again. Until then, you must not let our ways die and vanish away like so many of our people and our animal brothers have done."

"What am I to do father?" asked Screaming Hawk.

"You will be the keeper of our ways," replied the spirit. "You will teach your children and all the children of our tribe. Some will resist you on the reservation, but our ways must not die. All that is sacred to us must be cared for

Cottonwood
By Kevin J. Curtis

like a baby that is new to the world. You must feed it and help it to grow."

"The Great Spirit has told me that as sure as the four winds blow, the four races will one day come together. Our blood will be mixed with the blood of many others. When this happens, we will no longer be able to hate one another because of the color of the skin that holds our blood. All bleed red. But until that day, life will be difficult. Go now my son and teach the children what you have been taught. Keep our ways alive for those who are not yet born."

The spirit of his father rose, and walked back into the mist and was gone. Screaming Hawk tapped out his pipe and wrapped it back in the chamois and placed it back in the pouch around his waist. As he rose to go back to his canoe, an eagle flew over. The Bald Eagles' existence was also endangered, as the future held manmade toxins that would enter the environment. Screaming Hawk held his hand up and acknowledged the bird. The eagle, who flew closest to the Creator, had verified his new mission.

* * * *

Though the river valley was somewhat insulated from direct human influence, there were some major exceptions. One of these was the railroad. At the time that the railway was built, much of the work was done by hand, and much of the material was moved with horses. The work was hard and sometimes dangerous. Bridges were built across the water and sinking mud. Eventually, an earthen mound snaked right through the river valley. On top of this mound, the wooden ties held together the miles upon miles of steel tracks.

The railway provided a new means for people to transport goods, both in and out of the area. The trains ran back and forth through the river valley, and this made a

Cottonwood
By Kevin J. Curtis

huge impact on the environment as well. The river still provided for the transport of goods by barge, but the trains now ran year-round and day and night.

If one walked along these tracks with any frequency, he or she would find numerous animals that had become trapped or otherwise killed by the trains. There were deer, opossums, raccoons, huge snapping turtles and a variety of other animals that met their deaths beneath the wheels of the trains. Other animals, such as the wild turkeys, learned to find food on the railroad tracks. Many of the cars carried grain, and some of it was bound to escape, especially in the areas where the trains frequently stopped.

Among the unseen dangers, was the creosol used to help preserve the wooden ties. This was made with arsenic, which was a dangerous, long-lasting poison that was of course making its way out of the ties and into the environment.

The trains also started fires on occasion, as the steel wheels ran across the steel rails. This was intensified later, when the plants along the railway were chemically killed to clear them from the tracks. This dead plant material was good tinder for fires.

Fires were a part of the natural ecosystem and the benefits to the wilderness outweighed the damages. As humans settled the area, however, they found fire to be another natural enemy. The settlers organized firefighters and water brigades to keep the fires from destroying their houses and farms.

* * * *

The air was acrid and hazy. Smoke filled the sky over the bottomland forest. The prairie grasses were on fire and the hot summer wind blew the inferno along. The fire consumed the dry grass and burned the small trees of the forest. Some of the large oaks were able to withstand the

Cottonwood
By Kevin J. Curtis

searing heat until the available fuel was consumed and the fire passed by. In the path of the destruction, both plants and animals lay scorched in the wake of the flames. Later, after the destruction had passed, new life would sprout up; but now there was only fire and death.

One edge of the fire burned across the marsh where the cottonwood was growing. The tree had grown large, and the fire was impeded by the beaver pond and the river. Still, the tree was singed and the charred side that the flames had damaged became part of the cottonwood's history. The scarring would remain visible for years after until the tree finally grew around the wound and enveloped it with new tissue.

Up above, beyond the bluffs, the farms were in danger and all able-bodied men and boys were busy fighting the flames. They used shovels and hoes to dig trenches and mounds, and to pound out the burning embers.

Svenor was only 13, but he carried buckets of water from the creek to the men up front who were trying to keep the fire away from the barn. His brother was inside the barn leading the frightened animals out as the roof ignited and the hay inside reached its flash point.

The barn burned to the ground in minutes as the men frantically tried to keep the flames from reaching the house. The fire had its own cruel agenda as it devoured the farmhouse and was intent on crossing the wheat field to reach the neighboring farm. That was Svenor's father's farm!

Bravely the boy picked up a shovel and ran to head off the flames. He was nearly exhausted already from his many trips to the creek for water. As he ran toward his farm, the flames reached a frenzy and leapt upward into the sky. Smoke swirled all around him and soon the boy began to cough and choke. He couldn't see and he couldn't hear. He was disoriented and couldn't find his way out of the

Cottonwood
By Kevin J. Curtis

flames. He fell to the earth and felt the singeing of his hair against the scorched ground. The flames stung his body and his lungs were full of deadly smoke. Suddenly he felt himself being lifted toward the sky and everything went black.

The next day, tired and melancholy, family and neighbors waited, as the doctor looked at the boy who had been caught in the raging fire. When he emerged from the house, the doctor said that there was nothing more he could do. A few hours later, Svenor died from his burns and smoke inhalation.

Life was hard on these farms and fires were always a persistent threat. Medicine was still limited and the boy died at home. It was often customary to bury the dead in a family cemetery on the farm. In this case, Svenor was laid to rest in the cemetery of the church near town, next to his sister who had died from complications of a childhood disease. The plain wooden box was lowered into the ground, and the earth was mounded up around the top.

When the rains came later in the summer, the flowers that were planted on the grave mound began to bloom. The burned fields and woodlands began to green up. The neighbors all turned out (including Svenor's family), to rebuild the house and barn of the family who had been burned out.

Down below, in the river valley, the cottonwood was blackened on one side by fire. All around it, however, the new green leaves and sprouts were growing up through the black soil and ash, as life and death assumed their balance.

* * * *

Life on the farm was often defined by hard work. This was one of those late summer days that afforded some much needed recreational time. The spring and fall were

Copyright © 2008 by Kevin J. Curtis

Cottonwood
By Kevin J. Curtis

the busiest seasons on the farm. Winters were tough, and few were the lazy days of summer like this one.

The boys helped Grandma down to the levee below their house. The levee structure separated the two sides of the swamp. Where the water ran from one side into the other, it was a prime spot for fishing. Grandma would sit on the chair they brought for her and catch bullheads with a cane pole for the whole afternoon. That evening they would skin them and eat their fill of fresh fish.

The boys went squirrel hunting in the woods along the bluffs. Mostly they did this for sport, though they kept the hides and often ma would make a stew out of the meat. The two boys, ages eight and twelve, were already excellent marksmen. Part of this stemmed from the cost of bullets. They were not opposed to target practice; it was just that because of the cost of buying bullets, they preferred to make each round count.

On this day, even ma and pa had taken a lunch pail and rode the horse bareback up into the woods. They found a shady place beneath a swamp oak, and spread out their picnic for a relaxing lunch on an old blanket.

The dog, Shorty, was nearby. He had also found a cool spot in the shade and was asleep. Gus, the gelding ma and pa rode out on, was quietly munching grass. He was untied, but did not venture far away. All was serene on this sunny, summer afternoon.

The girls, ages nine and ten, were playing with homemade dolls that were made by grandpa, before he died last winter. He was buried up the hill; safe from the floods that frequented the farm most springs after the snow melted. Grandpa would have loved a day like today.

The boys had a squirrel apiece between them. The younger had shot a large Gray Squirrel and the older brother had killed a small Red Squirrel. The Red Squirrels were difficult to shoot because they were incredibly fast

Cottonwood
By Kevin J. Curtis

and they rarely stayed in one place for more than a few seconds. If the two boys weren't so skilled and patient in their hunting, they would not have been successful.

Grandma had a bucketful of bullheads by the time the boys came back for her. While they skinned their squirrels, grandma and the two girls began the long process of skinning bullheads. Soon the two boys started working on the fish as well, since there were quite a lot of them.

The bullheads were armed with sharp, stinging spines located on the dorsal fin and pectoral fins. Grandma could skin a bullhead in about two minutes. She expertly avoided the spines as she cut the skin and peeled it off of the fish. Then she cut out the fillets and tossed them into a bucket.

The two boys had devised another method. They had pounded an old, square nail through a board. With the pointed end up, they impaled the Bullhead's head onto the nail. This held the fish securely in place while they cut and peeled the skin loose and removed the meat.

By the time ma and pa came riding home on the horse, the first batch of fish were already crackling in the frying pan on the stove. The girls were cooking while grandma supervised close by. Meanwhile, the boys had dug a big hole and buried all the fish heads and entrails.

A big pot of boiled potatoes and the season's first crop of fresh corn complimented the meal. A table had been brought outside, to escape the summer heat. The whole family sat down together, and pa said, "grace" before the family passed around the food and started to eat. Everyone was in a good mood, which worked to the benefit of the dog and several cats that sat close to the table waiting for any less-than-desirable piece of food to be thrown their way. The animals also knew that they would be fed from what was left, as it was unheard of to buy dog or cat food in those days.

Cottonwood
By Kevin J. Curtis

After dinner, the two girls cleared the dishes and washed them. The two boys set to work feeding the animals. Pa took care of the horse, while ma milked the cow. Chores were finished before dusk, and the boys built a fire for the family to sit around. Evening brought a comfortable coolness as the sun banked behind the western sky. If it weren't for the mosquitoes, it would have been a perfect night.

Up above in the dark sky, a Nighthawk could be heard. Little Brown Bats exited the rafters of the barn and began flying erratically, searching for mosquitoes and other insects that they captured on-the-wing. As the moon came into view on the horizon, it looked huge. It had been a perfect day that was now becoming a perfect night.

* * * *

The cottonwood tree continued to grow in the mostly favorable conditions of the bottomland forest. One night, a raccoon waded into the marsh. It was a dark night. The sliver of moon had been completely blotted out by the clouds. The raccoon did not need the light. His sharp eyes were adept at seeing in the darkness. The animal worked in the shallow water until it found what it had come for. It was a carp that was struggling. The fish had reached the end of its life cycle.

This carp had spawned this spring for the last time, and now it was dying. Nature was very frugal, and the death of this fish would not be wasted. As the carp tried weakly to get away, the large raccoon dragged the big fish to shore. The masked hunter pulled the fish within a short distance from the growing cottonwood tree. The raccoon began to feast, and the carp gave up its life.

Carp had been brought to America from Europe not long before this fish began its life. The carp were very resilient, and had managed to survive and prosper in this

Cottonwood
By Kevin J. Curtis

new environment. Soon, the carp were taking over the territory of native fishes–just like what was happening with the people in North America at this point in history.

This fish had lived for sixteen years. During the time since it was a hatchling, it had lived in the river, and then in the marsh. The carp had spent several years in the murky shallows and the backwaters of the Minnesota River. When it spawned, it often swam upstream into the creeks and marsh ponds with others of its kind. Two years ago, the fish had grown too large to get out of the marsh. The beavers had dammed the stream and the fish was blocked from returning to the river.

The resilient carp had no difficulty making the marsh and beaver pond its new home. It had achieved a size that afforded it protection from most predators–including a persistent otter that frequented the marsh. Finally, it was the rigors of age that caused the carp to slowdown enough for the large raccoon to catch it.

The raccoon continued to crunch the flesh of the carp as it gorged itself on its meal. The night was filled with a variety of birds and animals that watched with interest. This was a large fish, and there would be leftovers. The raccoon finished, and ambled off into the night. It easily climbed into the cavity of a nearby cottonwood tree and disappeared.

As the remains of the carp lay unprotected, scavengers–including a coyote ate from it. By morning, little was left for the daylight scavengers. The soft tissue had been picked clean. Only the backbone and some scales remained in a small, rotting mound. Ants carried bits and pieces of the fish away. Some of the nutrients found their way through the soil, into the growing cottonwood tree. The tree was continuing the process on its journey to becoming one of the elders of the bottomland forest.

Cottonwood
By Kevin J. Curtis

* * * *

As more time passed and the cottonwood tree continued to grow, it eventually became one of many large trees in the bottomland. Still, it had not yet reached the huge size that would mark it as a monarch of the forest.

The periodic flooding in the river valley where it grew, protected it somewhat from the influence of human beings. Up above in the bluffs, however, it was a different story. Large manmade machines were being used to push down trees, fill in ponds and level hills. The landscape was being radically changed by humans to suit their needs.

Much of the landscape had been turned into farmland. Even some of the areas of the bottomland forest, in the floodplain, had been converted. The farmers here had decided that it was worth the almost yearly flooding in order to have the land that was deemed "unfit," and tax-free.

The animal life was either forced to flee from this destruction, or they were buried by it. Crops replaced the native plants, and the native animals were replaced by chickens, cattle, pigs and sheep. The delicate balance of nature was converted into the farmer's dung pile.

Still, down in the Minnesota River Valley, the remnants of nature were able to survive. Some things had obviously changed considerably. There were no longer many large animals–especially predators living there. One would have to go north or west to find these great creatures. There were still many animals and plants that were able to find some safety from man's influence by living in the bottomland forest. As time went on, however, there were many more hazards to the natural environment–both seen and unseen.

Cottonwood
By Kevin J. Curtis

Chapter 11: Leaving the Old Behind

The family had been farming in the area for about a generation when things suddenly began to change rapidly for them. They were German immigrants. Like most immigrants, they retained their language, some of their customs and food. Living primarily by subsistence farming, culture was not as important as what was practical. They had learned to use and do what worked best in order to put food on the table.

Now, early in 1942, life was about to change drastically. After the Japanese bombed Peal Harbor on December 7, 1941, a succession of events transpired that was beyond the control of the family, though it affected them profoundly.

On December 8th, the United States and Britain declared war on Japan. By December 11th, Germany and Italy declared war on the United States. The political and ideological battle between these countries caused this simple, farm family, to immediately and systematically abandon all ties to their native country.

Ingrid was only two years old, and did not yet understand what was taking place in her world. Her older siblings could speak their native German language, but they were no longer allowed to do so beyond the walls of their simple farmhouse. In fact, even their parents, Herman and Anna began using English exclusively from that point forward.

This was to an extent, an act of self-preservation. It was true that Japanese Americans were being rounded up and sent to internment camps. Also true, though to a lesser extent, Italians and Germans were also being sent to such places–especially if they had the audacity to continue practicing their traditions and native language.

Cottonwood
By Kevin J. Curtis

The farm was small by modern standards, at 40 acres.[7] Back in 1942, however, it was a decent size farm, able to support the two adults and their five children. Also within the parameters of the farm was the farmer's older brother, August. August had been born on the ship while sailing from Germany to America. Conditions onboard were deplorable, and it was no surprise that he had difficulty learning. Not much was known about developmental disabilities at the time, but Herman had built his brother a shack, so that he could live close by, in the woods just beyond the pasture.

The farm was comprised of a large vegetable garden, some fruit trees consisting of apples and cherries, wild raspberries, and a number of animals including, chickens, pigs, cows, sheep and horses. Dogs and cats would come and go, and life was difficult, as these animals were not the recipients of the type of food and medical attention that would be afforded to the pets of the years yet to come.

Beneath the house was a root cellar, with a dirt floor. This was where the family stored onions, potatoes, carrots, squash, apples and a variety of "canned" vegetables that were kept in glass Mason jars. The cellar was damp and cool year-round, and was the source of fear for the younger children. It was filled with creatures that enjoyed living in the cool darkness, such as spiders, centipedes, and even toads and salamanders.

There was no electricity on the farm, no telephone and the water came from a deep well, through a pump that was powered by a windmill. Stoves heated the house, and these burned oil that was purchased along with other commodities by surplus crops, animals and bartered labor, that was produced (by much manual labor) on the family farm. Horses still supplied much of the power for the farm,

Copyright © 2008 by Kevin J. Curtis

Cottonwood
By Kevin J. Curtis

though gasoline powered tractors were starting to become the new method of powering fieldwork.

The children attended a one-room schoolhouse, and they were (now) instructed by Herman and Anna, not to speak German but to use only English. There were other immigrants within the same area, most being originally from Ireland, Germany or various parts of Scandinavia.

During the next few years, the family became fully Americanized. While English became the only language that they now used, the adults still retained a thick German accent, punctuated by the reversal of the "W" and "V" sounds. This could be heard as Anna told Herman that the "wegetables were wery nice," or when he asked her, "Vhat are ve having for supper?"

Sitting in the Lutheran church one Sunday, the minister was speaking from the pulpit as usual. Little Ingrid sat on her mother's lap looking at the backs of the heads of everyone sitting in the pews ahead of her family. She was too young to know what was going on, but she was aware of the fact that the congregation in the church seemed upset by something.

Without modern sources to distribute the news, the church served as one resource to obtain information or news relevant to the community. The preacher was recounting the death of a member of the church. The young man, only eighteen-years-old, had died in Europe fighting in the war.

His family sat in the little church, and the men and boys were stone-faced as was expected of them. The young man's mother's eyes welled up with tears that betrayed her sorrow as she tried to remain strong. The fallen soldier's sisters cried softly and held on to each other.

The minister invited the congregation to attend a memorial for the young man later in the week. The body,

Cottonwood
By Kevin J. Curtis

he said had been buried in France, with many other Americans who had fought bravely for their country, and had died gallantly in battle.

It was but another reminder to Ingrid's family, of the strange position that they found themselves in. It was likely that their predecessors had fled Germany because of the difficulties that were now being contested in the Second World War. It was between World War I and World War II that they had arrived in America.

The current generation was not completely sure of all of the reasoning for the departure, and even if they were, they were often closed-mouthed about such things. The fear of what had happened and what was now being sorted out on the battlefields was strong enough to keep them cautious.

After church, Herman changed from his church clothes back into his denim coveralls that were his normal attire around the farm. The clothing and his body had a musty scent, as bathing was less frequent in those days due to the labor involved in carrying and heating the water.

He walked outside and past the chicken-coop to the shed adjacent to it. He opened the shed's door. Inside, was a distillery that was functional and was still periodically used to make homemade corn whiskey. The 'still was a remnant from prohibition, which had ended slightly less that a decade earlier. From 1920 until 1933, alcohol had been illegal. Over that time, many people had learned to make their own, and the product of this particular 'still was dubbed, "old chicken-coop."

Herman reached behind the wall and pulled out a chain. On the end of the chain was a metal jaw trap. When he removed it from behind the wall, he found that the trap held a large rat, now deceased from the crushing metal of the spring-loaded trap. He tossed the dead rat outside on the

Cottonwood
By Kevin J. Curtis

manure pile. He reset the trap, and baited it with a pinch of chickenfeed.

Then Herman reached behind the wall again, and this time he pulled out a glass jug. He removed the stopper, and took a large gulp of the brown liquid inside. He shook his head as the potent whiskey stung his mouth and throat. Then he put the stopper back into the jug and returned it to its place behind the wall.

"I reckon ve'll get through this," he said aloud, though no one was nearby to hear him. Then he left the shed, because there was always work to do on the farm.

Chapter 12: Things Seen and Unseen

The cottonwood tree continued to grow. It would be considered a large tree in most any woods, but it still had not yet reached the size of the giant cottonwoods of the bottomland forest. Many of these trees had roots stretching into the soft earth toward the water and sometimes reaching into the river itself. The result of this nutrient rich mixture was reflected in the enormous size of the trees.

The river contained not only beneficial nutrients, but also a variety of harmful toxins created by human beings. These chemicals were sometimes blatantly dumped into the waterways or on land to dispose of them. The river was also a favorite place for people to throw their trash, since it sank out of sight.

Regardless of whether it was buried or just dumped, the resulting pollution was often deadly to the wildlife living in the river or nearby. There was also another threat that was less blatant, yet perhaps even farther reaching in its deadly effects. Chemicals from household products, industry, medicine, and farming, were entering the environment. Sometimes they were visible, such as the "rainbow" left on the surface of a pond from petroleum

Cottonwood
By Kevin J. Curtis

products. Other times they were invisible to the eye, such as DDT runoff from farming or benzene from industry.

These and numerous other chemicals entered the environment in many ways. Often, these toxins would follow waterways and contaminate the rivers, lakes and groundwater. In the case of the pesticide known as DDT, it could eventually be detected everywhere in the world–including the most remote regions.

While they were able to escape many of the adverse effects of human occupation due to their ability to fly, birds were extremely susceptible to the negative effects that DDT exposure had to the quality of their eggshells. Most notable of the species that saw significant declines due to fragile eggshells, were the raptors. Most notable among the raptors, was the United States own emblem, the Bald Eagle.

Worse yet, was the fact that it would take the scientific community years to discover this danger, and longer yet for the public and government to finally cause changes to the business community that had become rich and gluttonous from its habit of polluting for the sake of maximizing profits. When DDT was finally banned in North America, it would take even longer for other countries to follow suit. Even after it was taken off the market, the chemical was still found for decades in the environment. Perhaps it would always be present in trace amounts forever after.

While this was all going on in the larger world, one late winter's day in the bottomland forest, the cottonwood tree had new tenants moving in. Branch by branch the eagles brought in materials and constructed an enormous nest in the heights of the large cottonwood tree. As was the case with raptors, the pair was mismatched in size opposite of most other birds and animals. The female was larger and more powerful than the male. Both had similar features and colors–including the white heads and tails that signified

Cottonwood
By Kevin J. Curtis

maturity. The white coloration occurred after about four seasons. Prior to that, the birds were a mottled brown.

The eagles worked on the nest until it was of sufficient size to accommodate the eggs that were soon to be laid by the female. If the pair returned the following year, they would add to the nest. After several successive years, it would become a gigantic structure that could support a human being. That is if someone were so bold as to climb up there. To come near to an active nest could mean incurring the wrath of a very large bird that was well armed with a hooked beak and powerful talons.

In this portion of history in the river valley, people were still not very good about allowing other predators to survive. Though humans hunted these woods and fished this river, the sight of another predator was cause for a man to begin shooting to rid the earth of another bear, fox, or even an eagle. In fact, at the time it was very common to shoot hawks, because of the real or perceived threat to chickens.

On this day though, the eagles were dominant and unmolested as they finished securing the branches of their nest. Soon, the female laid an egg and began to sit on it to keep it warm. Over the next two days, she laid two more eggs.

In order for a baby bird to develop and hatch, the egg needs to be kept warm and periodically rotated. Fortunately, eagles, like other animals, are born with the knowledge called instinct, to do the things that are necessary for survival. The problem occurred as the result of the DDT that been applied to the crops above the river valley, that had washed down into the river.

The DDT had ended up accumulating in the fish that lived in the river. Fish, are the primary and favorite food of Bald Eagles. So, when the eagles ate the fish, the

Cottonwood
By Kevin J. Curtis

DDT ended up inside of their bodies too. That means that the DDT also found its way into the eggs.

As the mother eagle gingerly used her hooked beak to rotate her eggs, the eggshell of the first one broke. It seems that when the eggshell dried and became hard, instead of providing *more* protection, it became fragile due to the effects of the DDT. Fragile eggshells made them break easily. After two more days, all the eggs had broken.

Now nature is somewhat resilient, and because of the quick demise of the eagles' eggs, the mother was able to lay one more a week later. For whatever reason, this particular egg was not quite as fragile, and perhaps the mother had become gentler in order to compensate. The eagle parents took turns sitting on the egg and as the weather began to warm up, a tiny new life emerged.

Baby birds, including the master of the sky, do not look too formidable when they first emerge from their eggshell. But soon, the nutrient rich food that her parents provided caused the young eaglet to grow rapidly. By late spring it was fledging. As the feathers grew in, she began to take on more of the look of an eagle. By early summer, she was standing on a branch near the nest with her wings outstretched, testing the air-currents.

Soon, the young eagle launched herself into the breeze and awkwardly pumped her wings up and down to gain lift. She moved higher and higher and then as instinct kicked in once again, she held her wings out from side to side and began to soar across the river like a huge glider. Still unsure of herself and having used muscles that she had never used before, the eaglet landed somewhat less than gracefully, into another large cottonwood tree across the river from the nest she was hatched in.

The mother and father eagle stayed close by for the next couple of months. They still continued to feed the young one, and they would fly to the rescue if any danger

Cottonwood
By Kevin J. Curtis

approached. Few enemies would risk an encounter with a ten pound[8] heavily armed raptor. By summer's end, the new eagle had a nearly seven-foot wingspan,[9] mottled brown color and was now able to fend for herself.

Not many eagles would reach maturity in the next few years and their numbers would decline so significantly, that they would be put on the U.S. Federal Government's *Endangered Species List.* This made the hunting or killing of an eagle illegal. Still, the species would remain endangered until long after the ban on the use of DDT.

Over the years, the same pair of eagles returned to the cottonwood tree each season to try again to successfully produce offspring. Over a five-year period, only one other eaglet made it to maturity. The fragile eggshells remained the most prominent threat to their survival. Though one other eaglet that did hatch, it was killed in a hailstorm that also severely injured the mother. The female eagle did not survive the winter due in part to her injuries. The male eventually moved on, and the nest remained vacant for a number of years.

On the ground below the cottonwood, the abandoned farm disc still rusted. By now, the tree had reached a diameter of about three feet.[10] During this time there were changes occurring on the inside of the tree. As was the norm for the huge cottonwoods in the bottomland forest, this tree had begun to rot out in the center. The tree was becoming hollow inside.

This was attractive to the inhabitants of the forest. Among the first to move in were the woodpeckers. The river valley was home to many varieties from Flickers, Hairy, Downey, Pileated, Red-headed and more. Though the tree was already home to numerous living things such as Carpenter Ants and other insects, the burrowing of the woodpeckers opened the interior of the tree to larger animals including owls, raccoons and various rodents.

Cottonwood
By Kevin J. Curtis

The huge Pileated Woodpecker hammered against the side of the cottonwood tree. Chunks of wood fell to the ground as the large woodpecker continued to assault the tree with quick successions of blows that could be heard throughout the woods for great distances.

The tree was so large now, that there was a tiny Downy Woodpecker also at work hammering in a much smaller and less noticeable way, elsewhere on the same tree. The difference in size between the two woodpeckers was quite remarkable. Still, they had the same basic mission. They chopped into the bark and wood of the huge tree in search of insects to eat. They also created nesting holes inside the trunk of the cottonwood.

This activity opened passageways into the hollow interior of the tree. Down below where the birds were working, a large cavity was visible and inside a mother raccoon had just given birth to four young. They were born quite helpless with their eyes closed. They would rely on their mother for all of their needs for the next few weeks.

Both inside and outside of the tree there were a variety of insects, worms and spiders. A tree frog lived on the outside of the tree, and could be heard chirping in the evening. A huge Wolf Spider had setup her web on a branch, and she enjoyed the benefits of the shelter and good trapping opportunities.

The spider sat motionless inside of a hole in the center of her web. A fly buzzed by, gracefully flying around the tree when it became entangled in one of the sticky web fibers. The spider felt the fly struggle and she ran out and bit into the fly's body with her fangs. She injected it with an enzyme that began to turn its insides into liquid. Then the tiny predator spun silk and wrapped the fly inside. She pulled her helpless prey back down into the hole in the center of the web, where she could suck its insides out at her leisure.

Copyright © 2008 by Kevin J. Curtis

Cottonwood
By Kevin J. Curtis

Inside of the tree's interior, a colony of Carpenter Ants had created a myriad of pathways throughout the tree. Some of the chambers held food, consisting of honeydew from aphids, plant juices and other insects. Other chambers were used to incubate eggs. There were chambers filled with larvae and workers caring for them. The colony was setup in a cast system, each member having been born into a specific job such as caring for the queen or the eggs and larvae, or as a general worker/forager. There were also certain ants that were larger. These were generally the soldiers, or the guardians of the colony. All of these ants were sterile females, except for two kinds with the jobs of reproduction.

The males, called drones, of which there were few, were tiny compared to the others. They had wings and only one purpose, to mate with the queen and fertilize the eggs. The queen was the reason the colony existed, though she was unable to survive on her own.

Deep inside of a center chamber, there was a huge white mass. One end of it had the much smaller head and thorax of a large ant. The abdomen, however, was enormous in comparison. The huge white abdomen pulsed as it laid eggs and worker ants retrieved, and brought them to an incubation chamber. The queen was once normal size, but now she was unable to move herself. She had become a giant egg-laying machine.

Twice each year, the colony would erupt with new queens, drones and workers, as they would emerge from the depths of the tree. The drones would fly off to either die, become prey for carnivorous insects, birds, reptiles or fish, or they would find a queen to mate with–at which point they would usually die soon after. The queens were also winged and if they could survive the hazards of the outside world, they would fly off to start new colonies. To do this, the queen would first pull her wings off. Then, after

Cottonwood
By Kevin J. Curtis

taking care of the first generation of her young, she would become a huge egg-laying machine that was cared for by successive generations.

Similar in nature to the ants, were the Bald-faced Hornets that made their large, grey paper nest that hung from a lower branch of the cottonwood tree. The nest was made from wood that was chewed up and mixed with saliva. The small, cone shaped chambers, provided space for eggs, larva and food, which was derived from plant nectar and arthropods[11] that the workers collected.

Each spring, young queens that had been fertilized by drones the previous year, would emerge from hibernating in the ground or in hollow trees. Then the queen would create the beginnings of a paper nest and lay the eggs that would hatch into infertile females that would become the workers and foragers. These workers would all possess a nasty stinger that they could use on anything that upset the nest. Unlike honeybees, the hornets were able to use their stingers multiple times.

While the colony structure and food of the ants and hornets were similar, the ant colony was over a decade old and the colony in the paper nest would die when winter came. Both colonies were made up of numerous individuals that worked together as if one organism. Both of these organisms had found different ways of ensuring the survival of their species from season to season.

Meanwhile, the baby raccoons in the cottonwood tree had passed a major milestone. After a couple of weeks their eyes were beginning to open. This was accompanied by an increase in their activity, though they were not yet ready to leave the safety of the hollow of the tree.

Drawn by the smell of mice that were also nesting in the bottom of the cottonwood, a large Bull Snake moved gracefully toward the base of the tree. The snake was large enough that the young raccoons were also in danger. The

Cottonwood
By Kevin J. Curtis

snake was a powerful constrictor that was able to coil its body around its victim and with strong muscles, suffocate the animal, bird or reptile.

As this snake moved in toward the mouse nest beneath the roots of the tree, it encountered an unexpected problem. The mother raccoon was in no mood to have such a large snake in the vicinity of her offspring. Nor was she adverse to making a meal of a snake if she was able to subdue it.

This particular snake was over six feet long[12] and was large enough that most predators would not bother it. A raccoon is an extremely tough animal for its size, and this female was fairly large. If she could sink her teeth into a vital spot on the snake, she could kill it. A snake of this size, however, was dangerous if it could wrap itself around the raccoon.

The raccoon struck first, and she grabbed hold of the snake with her hand-like front paws and then sunk her sharp teeth into its body. The snake struck at the raccoon and managed to bite her rear leg as it attempted to coil around its attacker. The raccoon leapt free, and backed away as the snake slithered away into the brush. The mother raccoon did not pursue. Each combatant was comfortable with letting the other go free.

Chapter 13: In and Around the Marsh

The most common snake in the bottomland forest and marshes was the Garter Snake. These snakes were usually much smaller than a Bull Snake, but in the rich habitat of the river valley, they could get quite large. There was ample food for these legless reptiles in the form of frogs, rodents, birds and even large insects.

The food chain extends in both directions for the majority of animals though, and one large Garter Snake

Cottonwood
By Kevin J. Curtis

emerged from the beaver pond at dusk with a mudpuppy in its mouth. Looking like a large salamander with gills, the mudpuppy was no match for the large snake and was in imminent danger of being swallowed. Along about this time, two young mink came chasing each other around the cottonwood tree and they ran right over the snake while it was trying to work its unhinged jaw over the thick body of the mudpuppy.

The mink each grabbed the snake, and the hapless serpent had no choice but to abandon its effort to eat its catch and attempt to struggle free. With a mink on each end, the snake could do little except endure the torture of being held by sharp teeth and stretched as the two mink pulled its body in a game of tug-o-war!

The two young mink made squeaks as they pulled with all of their might, each trying to free the prize from the other. They were so engrossed in their rivalry, that they did not notice the large, Barred Owl dive out of the trees on top of them. With wings flapping and sharp talons raised, the owl slammed down on one of the mink and drove those deadly talons into the animal with incredible power. The mink thrashed momentarily and then succumbed to its wounds and the strength of the owl.

The second mink and the snake both escaped while the first mink was being further assaulted by the sharp, strong, talons and beak of the raptor. With its prey now subdued, the owl flapped furiously until it was able to lift both itself and the dead mink upward into the trees. A strange silence now engulfed the woods, as no birds or animals were making any noise. All were listening intently, waiting for the danger to pass before resuming their lives.

On the other side of the river, one of the most powerful raptors had laid claim to what had formerly been a hawk's nest. The Great Horned Owl was sitting with three fuzzy owlets. She had just driven another owl away

Cottonwood
By Kevin J. Curtis

that had come too close. The feathers that lay strewn about on the ground below the tree were the only evidence that still remained from the fight.

Her mate was close by. He had been successful hunting tonight. He had found a Striped Skunk wandering through the woods, and on silent wings, the owl had sailed out of the trees and onto it. After killing the skunk and returning to the trees, the owl swallowed the animal whole.

Now, still sitting in the tree, he regurgitated the hair and some bones and teeth in pellets that dropped to the ground beneath him. Those parts that were difficult to digest were disposed of in this way. This was characteristic of all owls, though the Great Horned Owl was one of the only animals that were known to routinely eat skunks. These large birds seemed to be immune to both the skunk's smell and the rabies that were frequently carried by these animals.

From across the dark marsh, the sound of a Barred Owl was carried on the night air. The call sounded as if the bird was saying, "Who cooks for you? Who cooks for you all?"

Back at the cottonwood tree, a Little Brown Bat was just returning home from hunting insects on the wing. The only mammal capable of true flight, the bat could devour hundreds of insects in a single night. With the prevalence of mosquitoes in this marsh and woods, these small creatures were both well fed, and also beneficial in reducing the numbers of the tiny insect-vampires.

The mosquitoes were so abundant in the warm summer months, that a person walking in this area at night would be covered by them. The sheer quantity and voraciousness of these insects made them a serious threat to anyone who was not wearing protective clothing.

The mosquito larva started out living in the water of the marsh. They lived just below the surface with a tube,

Cottonwood
By Kevin J. Curtis

like a snorkel, sticking just above the surface of the water so they could get air. Dragonfly larva, small fish and many other insects and animals ate the mosquito larva, but once again, the sheer numbers of these insects was such that they were in no danger of disappearing.

Also in the water were tadpoles. These were the young of frogs and toads, which had laid their eggs in the waters of the marsh and the beaver pond. The tadpoles that emerged from the eggs appeared more like fish to begin with. Gradually, they developed limbs and lost their tails– that is, if they were able to avoid predators long enough for these changes to take place.

Such was the story of life and death within the marsh. The plants and animals seemed to be on a never-ending scale that went ever smaller, and perhaps ever larger. As the life forms got smaller, their world became larger. The enormous quantity of life in these small realms was staggering to the mind. All seemed interdependent, and the microorganisms seemed to be the driving force behind the entire (larger) ecosystem. How astounding to think that the survival of the deer or coyotes that roamed these woods was dependent on tiny, single-cell life forms; but it was true.

Also true were the far-reaching effects that the toxins produced by these organisms could have. Humans were now contributing poisonous substances to the ecosystem as well. Toxins produced by plants like Blue-green Algae, or those that were produced by humans could upset this delicate balance of life and death. Such toxins could kill off entire populations, which might in turn cause the overpopulation of some other species. This would upset the balance that naturally occurred between the destroyed or overpopulated organisms and those that used them for food or were preyed upon by them.

Cottonwood
By Kevin J. Curtis

Some of these changes occurred as the result of *natural selection,* and others occurred because of the effects of mankind's waste and manipulation of the environment. As human influence increased in the vicinity of the bottomland forest, the resulting waste products found their way into the soil and water of the area. Certain plants and animals began to disappear, and others, sometimes those introduced by man (such as the European Carp), took over and began to displace the native species.

Nature is both resilient and fragile. While it is easy for these changes to wipeout an entire species, other organisms seem to be able to thrive. Some, like Turkey Vultures, actually like human garbage. Since they are adapted to consuming dead and decaying animals, vultures often hang around where humans dump their garbage. Many other animals have adapted to this as well. Rats that traveled with humans from Europe and other countries, established themselves in the cities that developed. Their numbers grew rapidly as the human population of cities grew. These same rodent pests were often responsible for carrying the deadly diseases that spread throughout human civilizations. Even many of these diseases were transplants from Europe or other faraway places.

Still, some of the local animals were able to thrive. As human cities grew larger, development would push the animal population out of their habitat. Some animals like many birds, rabbits, Grey Squirrels, foxes, coyotes and deer, learned to live in areas inhabited by human beings. Since hunting was usually restricted in cities, the animals that learned to use parks and backyards as homes were able to survive.

Places like the marsh and bottomland forest were buffers between the urban areas and the wilderness. All sorts of wildlife could live in the river valley. Some of these animals were unable to take up permanent residence

Cottonwood
By Kevin J. Curtis

in human cities and towns, but they would occasionally wander into the areas inhabited by humans.

Shamefully, even in more modern times the usual way of dealing with these animal encounters was to shoot the animal dead. This practice seemed to have become the norm even if the animal was a threatened species. In the name of public safety, the millions of human beings were protected from the single moose, bear or cougar that happened to wander onto a road or into a park or backyard. Some human ways of thinking are shortsighted and hard to change. When we take this into consideration, we can see why people did the things they did a century or two ago.

* * * *

As the morning sun cast shadows over the marsh, the nocturnal animals settled in and the songbirds were the first to greet the new day. The crickets hid beneath rocks and logs, and the sun warmed the grasshoppers until they literally sprung into action.

The nighttime moths hid in cracks and crevices and the butterflies warmed their wings in the morning sunshine before taking flight. They landed on summer flowers to drink the nectar with their long proboscises.[13] Honeybees were also warmed into action, as they visited the Hawkweed, thistles and Ironweed flowers that bloomed in the open areas. Mounds of fresh soil indicated the presence of gophers at work, and the buzzing of deerflies now took over from the mosquitoes that retreated into the shadows.

The Red Fox carried an American Woodcock back to her kits that were playing near their underground den. The four curious pups tugged at the woodcock she dropped on the ground for them. They began to play tug-o-war, and practiced sneaking up on it. This play would help build the

Cottonwood
By Kevin J. Curtis

muscles and skills these young foxes would need to hunt for themselves.

Up, over the bluffs at the farm nearby, the male fox had not made it through the night. Woken up by the sound of chickens and his dog barking, the farmer had managed to direct a shotgun blast at the fox, just as he emerged from the hen house with a limp chicken dangling from his mouth. By morning, he was skinned and hanging out to dry on the farmer's fence.

Back down in the river valley, a Virginia Opossum wandered slowly along the edge of the beaver pond. The 'possum was a southern animal that was beginning to expand its range. The hairless ears and tail of the only North American marsupial were prone to frostbite in the cold winters here in the Minnesota River Valley. Still, this was southern Minnesota, and the opossums were utilizing burrows in the ground, and nests in hollow trees to avoid the frigid temperatures. They were not traditionally found this far north, however, and a sighting was still somewhat rare.

Also rare was the American Badger. These vicious little carnivores were found all over Minnesota, but they were rarely seen. Could one of the large burrows frequently found in the river valley belong to one of these animals? Perhaps, though such a burrow might belong to something else, like a woodchuck.

Woodchucks were large marmots that were quite common throughout the region. While they seemed to like to build their burrows near open areas that provided for the grasses and small plants they preferred, they could also be found occasionally climbing in trees. These large rodents could provide food for the resident carnivores, though they were often prone to fighting back, and pound per pound they were extremely vicious.

Cottonwood
By Kevin J. Curtis

Along the river, marsh and beaver pond, stately Blue Herons waded in the water. More obvious were the white colors of the Common Egrets. Both of these birds had been hunted relentlessly by humans for their beautiful plumes. Though people would come to the bottomland to hunt, the area afforded habitat to these large wading birds, and the trees were often filled with their nests.

Heron colonies of both egrets and Great Blue Herons could sometimes boast hundreds of nests in a few dozen trees. In the summer, the ground below these congregations was littered with bird droppings and feathers. In the winter, when the leaves fell off of the trees, the nests were visible and the sheer quantity of them was something to behold.

Also present were Green Herons, Night Herons and Least bitterns. These birds were sometimes hard to distinguish one from the other. The bird life was spectacular none-the-less, and many more were visible on the river.

Double Breasted Cormorants swam in the swift river currents and then dried their wings by holding them outstretched while perched on logs or rocks. Pied-billed Grebes with their necks snaking up out of the water looked like miniature versions of the cormorants.

The resident ducks were Mallards, Wood Ducks and Canada Geese, though migratory ducks seen on the river in spring or fall included, Teal, Golden Eyes, Scaup and Mergansers.

In the trees, crows, Blue Jays, Chickadees, and sometimes Cardinals frequented the woods where the cottonwood grew. Summer residents included Red-winged Blackbirds, Robins, finches and Baltimore Orioles.

Even though human influence had reduced the diversity of life in the river valley, there was still an enormous amount of it. If one were to try to categorize all

Cottonwood
By Kevin J. Curtis

of the diversity, it would take more than a lifetime. Even the number of different types of moss or algae was impressive. The wildflowers alone would take at least a whole growing season to compile, since there was always something different in bloom depending on the time of the year.

So, while the influence of man had made an impact on the life found in the river valley, the bottomland forest was protected from many of the direct changes that human beings made. While there was some farming in the river valley, the periodic flooding kept most construction and human habitation up above the valley. The result was an area rich in natural wonders that had managed to escape much of the construction and direct manipulation of human beings.

Chapter 14: Linear Time

Time is said, to be a manmade concept. In the wilderness, the seasons come and the seasons go. Animals and plants live and die and more animals and plants come after them. Humans retain the concept of individuality. When a specific person lives and then dies, that lifetime is said to have covered a certain span of time, or a certain number of years.

The Earth runs on a 365 ¼ day, year, and there are actually thirteen cycles of the moon. Western culture has abandoned the number thirteen for superstitious reasons, and developed a twelve-month year with irregular numbers of days in the months.

The American Indians, who lived in the Minnesota River Valley before the Europeans came, did not have such superstitions regarding the number thirteen. As a matter-of-fact, thirteen was an important number to their culture. The Indians recognized that not only did the moon have thirteen

Cottonwood
By Kevin J. Curtis

cycles in a year, but so did women. They also recognized thirteen in other parts of nature, such as the thirteen sections in a turtle's shell.

Stephen Hawking would later come up with the concept of *imaginary time,* which runs at right-angles to "real-time." There are many more interesting ideas about this subject, but suffice to say, the cottonwood that had been growing for so many years in the river valley, was approaching the end of its life. It now had a diameter of over four feet.[14] It was at last, a true monarch of the bottomland forest. These trees live approximately ninety years, and this one was still relatively healthy, despite its advanced age.

It was late in the spring, when this old tree began to release its seeds into the wind. The seeds were carried on the trademark cotton that gave the tree its name. One particular seed landed in the soft soil near the bank of the river, not far from the giant cottonwood it had come from.

This seed, like many others, found itself struggling to start life. There was an element of luck involved. The right conditions needed to exist, and the first hours, days and months were critical. If a dry-spell occurred when the seed was germinating, or right after it started growing, it might wilt and die. If there was a flood, it might get washed away into the river. Many hazards were possible between this early time, and the potential future of reaching around ninety feet tall.[1]

This seed had found a good place to begin its life, near to the bank of the Minnesota River. This resting-place could prove beneficial, as the areas near the banks of the river were always well watered and nourished–even in a year of drought. There were risks though, too. Even a large tree could break loose in the soft soil, and topple during a storm or flood.

Cottonwood
By Kevin J. Curtis

One such example of this was not far from where the tree was beginning its new life. There, in the forest, was a long double-row of giant trees that had tipped over. The two rows were in parallel lines that extended for some distance, so that it included about ten, very large trees. If one was to examine their dilemma, he or she might come to the conclusion that it must have been straight-line winds.

That, however, would leave the question as to why the trees had fallen down this double-row, uniformly in the opposite direction of the opposing single row. In each parallel line, the trees had fallen away from the other line, with their roots facing toward each other. What then could have uprooted these trees? They were too far away from the river for the flood currents to be that strong. Could it have been a tornado? The other trees nearby seemed unaffected, so this might *seem* like the obvious answer.

Now if one was very astute, and liked to think about all of the possibilities, one-by-one in his or her mind, a very likely scenario might once again point to straight-line winds. The answer to the unique positioning of the uprooted trees could be explained by a "lever" action.

As one line of trees was pushed over by straight-line winds, with their roots breaking free in the soft, wet soil, they would pull up and out. As they fell, they would create a lever action against the trees in the line next to them, pulling against the roots on one end, and effectively levering them loose to fall down in the opposite direction. The end result would be the double line of trees that were toppled over, with each tree having fallen the opposite way as the one in the line parallel to it.

This was a unique sight that might not be repeated in this area for a very long time. Yet, if one was to consider the incredible length of *linear time* that passed in the creation of the bottomland forest, it was very likely that this

Cottonwood
By Kevin J. Curtis

was not the first time that this phenomenon had taken place.

Not all of the changes that occurred over time in the river valley were natural. Human settlements demanded power and fuel. To accommodate this need, a coal-burning electrical power plant was built in the 1950's. It was near the river to provide for the coal needed to produce electricity to be brought in by barge. On the other side of the new facility, railroad tracks also provided access for coal. The plant had been built on the edge of a lake, and the waters of this lake were used to cool its machinery. This in turn, caused *heat pollution* in the lake. The lake and the power plant were both named, *Black Dog,* after an American Indian chief who had once lived in the area.

The warmed waters of Black Dog Lake did not freeze entirely over the winter. This open water drew all sorts of migratory waterfowl, such as ducks, geese, cormorants, pelicans and swans. Sometimes these birds stayed for the entire winter instead of migrating south. The heated water was unfit for many fish, and the dominant species became the rough fish such as carp and bullheads.

Huge metal supports were built to hold power-lines above the ground, and these were diverted to a myriad of smaller poles, lines and substations throughout the area. One could hear the sizzle of high voltage going through the power-lines–especially when there was a light rain or when snow was falling. It would not be until later, when scientists would recognize the effects of *electromagnetic waves,* or frequencies, also called EMF's. Still, any such dangers were given little thought if they weren't near human dwellings.

Another change implemented by utility companies was the *natural gas* lines that were dug underground throughout the river valley. One of these gas lines was buried beneath Black Dog Lake. The construction of these

Cottonwood
By Kevin J. Curtis

utility lines definitely upset the environment when they were being installed. Nature was determined; however, to grow back over the damages, but maintenance crews returned routinely to push nature back when it got too close.

There were limited roads that passed through the bottomland, and then crossed over bridges to the opposite side of the river. These roads were prone to flooding each spring when the snow melted and the runoff swelled the banks of the river. Sometimes they also flooded after a severe storm or an extended spell of wet weather. As the human population grew, increased traffic caused more pollution in the river valley.

Another influence on the area was the international airport. Air traffic was often diverted over the natural areas, to keep the noise away from people's neighborhoods. The airport and airplanes were also a source of toxins that found their way into the environment.

Not all of the changes were bad though. Some of them were more of a political nature, such as when vast areas of the bottomland were designated as the Minnesota Valley National Wildlife Refuge in the year 1976. Ironically, the headquarters of this wildlife refuge was built in close proximity to the international airport.

Now placed under the management of the U.S. Fish & Wildlife Service, much of the land and water of the Minnesota River Valley was designated for wildlife and limited recreational use–including some hunting. The service also started a program of *controlled burns,* to revitalize prairies, Oak Savannah and to eliminate excess dead plant material. Water control structures were built both to reduce flooding, and to create wetlands for birds and other animals.

Another exciting prospect, was the fact that for the first time, land was actually being taken out of private

Cottonwood
By Kevin J. Curtis

ownership and farming, and given back to wildlife. This was a new course of action for the human population, as some people began to feel a sense of loss over the natural habitat that had been destroyed and a desire to save some of the wild areas for future generations began to develop. Around this same time, the area around the Black Dog Power Plant was leased long-term, to the Minnesota Valley National Wildlife Refuge.

The post-Vietnam War era also gave rise to other wrongs being set right. The Freedom of Religion act was implemented in 1978, just as Screaming Hawk's father's spirit had revealed to the young warrior almost a century before it happened. It was now legal for American Indians to openly practice their spirituality. By this time, however, either the Native Americans were absorbed into the cities and towns of the larger population, or they were still living on the reservations that they were pushed onto roughly a century earlier.

Other notable dates that benefited the original inhabitants, included 1967, when Bald Eagles were declared an endangered species (south of the 40th parallel) by the United States Federal Government. This preceded the *Endangered Species Act* of 1973. In 1974, wolves were added to the Endangered Species list. By this time, however, wolves were long gone from the bottomland forest and the human population was not likely to welcome them back. Regardless, the U.S. Fish & Wildlife Service introduced a recovery plan for the wolves in 1978. By 2007, wolves would be removed from endangered status, after a remarkable recovery in northern Minnesota. Later that same year, Bald Eagles would also be removed from the endangered list, as pairs of nesting birds reached sufficient numbers.

Eventually, during the expansion of the mid-twentieth century, the number of human inhabitants had

Cottonwood
By Kevin J. Curtis

grown significantly. They had built houses above the river valley. Neighborhoods of houses now sat where the farms had previously been. Some of the largest houses overlooked the river valley. The people who lived there needed access across the river to work in the many businesses that had developed in the area over the years.

There came a time, when the bridges were no longer acceptable and new ones were built. The new bridges were huge in comparison to those they replaced. They had multiple lanes and could handle much more traffic. Even more important, was that they spanned long distances over not just the river, but also the land nearby that was prone to flooding.

Of course, this had an impact on the river, the marsh, the wildlife and the bottomland forest itself. In some cases, lakes were destroyed by the construction, and marsh was left behind. Enormous pilings were sunk into the ground and then concrete reinforced with steel was used to create the monstrous bridges. The new bridges shaded the areas beneath, and some plants thrived, while others were deprived of the sun they needed.

Swallows built their mud nests on the sides and undersides of the bridges. The humans that used the bridges threw things out of their cars or portions of their loads were lost on the bridges. The vehicles also dripped oil, gas and antifreeze onto the bridge decks. All of this pollution eventually found its way down below into the waters of the marsh, the river and in the woods. The trees had plastic bags hanging in them, and a variety of garbage and pieces of vehicles littered the land and water below.

Some of the wildlife was resilient, and could live in the manmade watersheds that drained into the marsh and the river. Other times, these water basins were so filthy, that they were littered with dead ducks and rotting fish that

Cottonwood
By Kevin J. Curtis

had been poisoned. This, unfortunately, would become a constant menace to the environment below the bridges.

One could find wrappers from fast-food restaurants, tires, paper and beverage cans and bottles. There seemed to be no end to the garbage. When the floodwaters came each spring, these items were all carried by the water into the marsh, woods and river.

In collaboration with the Minnesota Department of Natural Resources, the U.S. Fish & Wildlife Service and private groups had many projects to help improve wild habitat. This included restoration of waterfowl production areas, cleaning up litter and trying to reestablish native plants.

Some plants that were originally introduced by the human settlers, had become invasive and had taken over many of the wild areas–including some of the areas within the Minnesota River Valley. Notable among these, was buckthorn and Purple Loostrife. Both of these plants had become problematic over the years. Much time, money and effort was directed toward their eradication.

Buckthorn was a prime example of an exotic plant that had begun to take over. It grew in thick hedges that crowded out the native species. An aquatic equivalent to this was Eurasian Water Milfoil, which was originally used as an aquarium plant. Later it got into the local waterways and was transferred on boats to more and more lakes where it became overgrown.

Other changes that had been instigated by man included the building of the Blue Lake Waste Treatment Plant in 1970. This facility treated the sewage generated by the many humans living in the area. This treated water was slowly released into Blue Lake and the Minnesota River. This discharge kept the water open in these areas during the winter.

Cottonwood
By Kevin J. Curtis

In the river, eagles congregated near the discharge flow. Other migratory birds could often be found there as well. Around Blue Lake, there were areas of mud and water that stayed open year-around. Robins were known to winter there, rather than to fly south. The wet, unfrozen earth provided a rich habitat for earthworms that provided a good supply of food for the birds.

Also in the area, was a huge "sanitary" landfill that was in operation since 1962. Because of the increase in human population and the waste produced, this landfill grew larger each year. Buried in the ground, was all sorts of solid waste generated by human beings. Though covered over by dirt, it would forever be a source of methane gas discharge and toxins that would find their way into the surrounding environment. This was the best that people had come up with to dispose of their waste.

Many changes occurred over time. The new cottonwood tree began to take root and grow along the river where its seed first germinated. Meanwhile, the older tree that the seed had come from was dieing. The inside of the tree was hollow and rotting. The branches were broken off and most were now without leaves. Time had taken its toll, and this tree was nearing the end of its life. The species lived on, however, as the new tree was just beginning its life journey.

It was not a journey across distances, but rather, across time. These trees were stationary by the laws of nature. Yet the surrounding area teamed with life. The great trees were witnesses to the many changes that occurred over linear time.

Of course, some of the hardwoods lived even longer than the cottonwoods did. They were unable, however, to reach the enormity in size that the cottonwoods could achieve. Cottonwoods, it seemed, were the products of their environment. One that might be found growing in the

Cottonwood
By Kevin J. Curtis

desert sands of the southwestern United States would likely be quite small compared to one growing in the moist and nutrient rich Minnesota River Valley. The enormous size of the older cottonwoods in the valley, made them hard to ignore.

While some trees could live very long lives, the trees of the river valley were "new" in comparison to certain other natural features. As to what was the oldest, or largest feature of its kind, that distinction went to the *Sand Creek Prayer Stone,* which was undoubtedly the largest single rock lying above ground in the (Louisville Swamp unit of the) Minnesota Valley National Wildlife Refuge. This huge piece of basalt was probably around two-billion years old. It had been left in the open by a long gone glacier.

What stood out in regard to the cottonwood trees, was that such huge living things existed here, and despite their size and age, they were just "passing through" life as anyone else who was mortal would do.

Chapter 15: Storms, Death and New Arrivals

In the woods near the new cottonwood tree, a flock of Wild Turkeys made its way past. The large birds foraged for seeds and insects. They were also fond of acorns in the fall. These birds rarely flew, though when startled they were quite capable of short flights. At night, they often roosted high in the trees to stay away from predators such as coyotes. The feathers of the turkeys were beautiful in color. The wing feathers were brown and white striped. The tail feathers were reddish and the sides of the birds were often a black and iridescent green color.

Wild turkeys had made a remarkable comeback. Few and far between when the cottonwood that was now dieing first emerged from its seed, the large birds had later

Cottonwood
By Kevin J. Curtis

disappeared completely because of over hunting. They were no longer seen in the bottomland forest. Reintroduced later by man, the large birds slowly began populating, as the pressure from hunting was greatly diminished.

No longer did people rely on hunting and farming for their food. The small, family farm was becoming a thing of the past. Large farms now produced surplus food that was trucked to warehouses and then to grocery markets throughout the area. This meant that hunting and farming were no longer the primary occupations or the main way of supplying food and clothing to your family. People now held jobs in services and industry and bought their food at supermarkets.

The new cottonwood seedling blew softly back and forth in the early summer breeze. Nearby, a dragonfly nymph was emerging from the marsh. It had spent its larval stage below the surface of the water hunting for smaller animals, insects, tadpoles and fish. This one was a Green Darner, which was a common, though rather large dragonfly.

The nymph had used its labium, or lower mouthpart to snare its prey. Both the larva and the adult were voracious predators. This nymph was about to go thorough a transformation that would take it to new heights. While in the larval stage the nymph may have been aquatic, but as an adult it would soar through the air and take its prey on the wing.

After crawling to a suitable spot, up out of the water on a cattail stem, the insect's back began to split open. As it slowly emerged from its old skin, two pairs of translucent wings unfolded. After drying in the sun and the light breeze, the insect took flight. There was no learning period. It could fly as soon as its wings were dry. Instinct had supplied this insect with all it needed to know.

Cottonwood
By Kevin J. Curtis

The dragonfly had changed little since prehistoric times. Back then, however, some of these insects were absolutely enormous by modern standards. Still, the body shape had remained virtually unchanged.

The insect landed on the new cottonwood tree. Its wings rested horizontally, which was characteristic of a dragonfly. Damselflies rested their wings upright. After a few minutes, it took flight once again, and easily captured a mosquito as it flew over the river. The dragonfly used its powerful mouth, to bite off the wings of the mosquito before devouring it while still airborne. During its lifetime, this same scenario would be repeated thousands of times.

As the summer progressed, the new cottonwood tree managed to avoid the many hazards, which could have prevented it from surviving. Meanwhile, not far away, the giant old cottonwood tree was clinging to the last remnants of its life.

By midsummer, the weather had become hot and dry. The tiny cottonwood struggled against the lack of moisture. The hardship left a mark on the core of the tree, as it slowed its growth and hung onto life.

Nearby, the old cottonwood was beyond needing water during a drought. Its roots stretched down into the ground and even reached into the beaver pond. Its feebly leafed branches were not starving for moisture. Water was not the problem for this tree, not yet anyway.

A robin chirped the song it normally sang as the day grew dim and the evening set in. Only, it wasn't evening yet. The sky was becoming prematurely dark as a storm moved into the area. The light breeze betrayed what was about to come, as the rumble of thunder could be heard moving in from the northwest.

The world looked strange, as the greenish light was skewed by the thick black wall of clouds that came roaring

Cottonwood
By Kevin J. Curtis

in like a freight train. The bird had stopped its song, and all the animals braced for the coming storm.

In minutes, it was there, thundering through the river valley. Periodically the darkness would be lit up like midday, with a flash of lightning. Hail began to fall, along with a deluge of rain. The water hit the parched ground and began to run off. It would take a few minutes for the soil to begin to accept the soaking raindrops, and the first of it ran in currents across the ground to the lowest points and into the waterways.

Huge shock waves of sound rumbled across the river valley as the thunder and lightning increased. One lightning bolt hit a large cottonwood across the river. The electricity split the outer bark and ran down the tree to the soil beneath, leaving a burn mark from top to bottom. This tree would survive the huge jolt of electricity, but beneath it lay a few small songbirds that had been killed in the process.

As the hail began to subside, the rain increased and the temperature had now dropped significantly. The heat of a few minutes ago was crushed by the cold wind and falling ice from the sky.

The falling rain and rushing water had now penetrated the soil. While the tiny, new cottonwood tree held firmly to the riverbank, it was replenished by the moisture. Nearby, however, the old cottonwood was beginning to lean as the wet ground around it started to give away.

During the full fury of the storm, the old monarch of the bottomland forest fell down. Loud cracks could be heard as the roots were pried up and broken as the weight of the old tree levered them loose. Upon impact, the limbs of the old tree shattered against the ground. The inside of the old tree was now exposed. Rotting wood shown in chunks as the rain matted them down.

Cottonwood
By Kevin J. Curtis

As the rain soaked into the fallen tree, the inside looked red in the angry, pale light of the storm. As if it was bleeding real blood, the rain droplets ran red down the rotting insides. Perhaps the blood carried memories of the days, and years that had passed. Perhaps the residue of all who had come in contact with the tree, or all who had bled where it grew was now released into the world and carried away by water; the Earth's blood.

After a few more minutes, the storm moved off to the southeast. Steam rose off of a nearby boulder, attesting to the temperature change that had just occurred. The trees and plants dripped with life-giving water as the drought had now been broken. Here and there, a few large trees had either lost branches in the wind, or had been toppled to the ground by the strong winds and loosened soil.

The old cottonwood lay prone and broken on the ground. There was nothing left now except for the forces of nature, of rot and breakdown, instigated by minute organisms. This tree had reached the end of its life. It had struggled against age, and all at once it had been toppled to the forest floor.

* * * *

They were driving home in their 1965 Pontiac Catalina from Grandma and Grandpa's house. The car was roomy, but the two brothers fought in the backseat anyway. There was an imaginary line down the middle, and when the younger brother crossed it, his brother hit him in the shoulder. The younger one was fairly helpless to enforce the rule when his older brother invaded his territory.

The family of four was all in the car, along with their dog. It was a small dog, and it was able to squeeze between the door and the seat to get from the front to backseat. Once in back, the dog exerted its dominance and claimed the roomy back window. The small terrier mix

Cottonwood
By Kevin J. Curtis

jumped onto the ledge beneath the back window and rode with the wind whipping through its hair.

The car had a 389 cubic inch (6.37 liters) V-8 engine, and it purred down the two-lane blacktop with little effort. They were headed north across the small two-lane bridge that spanned the Minnesota River, before crossing Long Meadow Lake to get back home.

There was a storm moving in from the north at an alarming speed. The small bridge shook in the wind, and the water below frothed as the storm hit in full fury just as the car was halfway across. The bridge was too narrow to pull off to the side, and it was not where you would want to be in a storm anyway.

Their dad was behind the wheel, and the two boys knew that he could get them out of this mess. He had to slow down as the rain and then hail slammed against the windows, but he kept the Catalina moving slowly, hoping that no one had stopped on the bridge in front of him. Eventually when he reached the far end of the bridge, the prudent thing to do was to pull over on the side of the road to wait out the full fury of the storm's blast.

When the hail stopped, and the rain slowed enough to see with the windshield wipers working on high, the driver pulled the Catalina back onto Cedar Avenue and headed toward home.

Meanwhile, the rain continued to pour down and the surrounding area drained into the basin that was the Minnesota River Valley. The water below the bridge kept rising as the rain continued. Low areas were already underwater, and the water level began to come dangerously close to the bridge deck.

The sky opened up for several hours and when it finally stopped, it took several more hours before the water level peaked. The rainwater from all over the area drained into ponds, watersheds and eventually into the lakes and

Cottonwood
By Kevin J. Curtis

rivers. The lowland filled with an enormous volume of water. In the end, there were plants hanging from the girders of the bridge, showing how high the water had been.

* * * *

Near the river, the new cottonwood was sporting a new shade of green as the life-giving moisture entered its being. In fact, the entire forest seemed to be a shade or two greener than it had been just before the storm arrived.

A tree was carried past on the swollen current of the Minnesota River. The water was darkened from the runoff of the storm. In a few places, the river was flowing over the banks. As the river and rainwater flowed into the marsh, the waters there rose as well. The old road was now submerged, and a large carp was fighting against the swift current running across it.

Soon, the clouds parted and the sun shone again. The harsh rays beat against the soggy earth and both the temperature and the humidity began to rise. Flies started to buzz, and the mosquito eggs that had been lying dormant in the dry soil since the last flood, began to incubate.

Before too long, mosquito larva were wriggling around in the rainwater ponds. The larva stayed near the surface, where breathing tubes located in the abdomens of the insects, were pushed above the surface of the water. On the head end of each insect, small brush-like appendages helped the developing mosquito to capture microscopic plants and animals for food. After changing into pupae, these developing mosquitoes could be seen swimming through a small rainwater pond, using their tail appendages to propel them.

When the adults began to hatch, the males used plant nectar for food, while the females searched for blood. The hungry females would suck blood from any animal that

Cottonwood
By Kevin J. Curtis

they could find. Unfortunately, when they moved from one animal (or person) to the next, they could carry diseases from one to the other.

One of these hungry mosquitoes happened to be carrying a virus, when it found a Blue Jay. The small flying insect hovered around the bird until it found a suitable place to land. It managed to find a place to stick in its proboscis, and it injected a small amount of fluid into the bird, which among other things, helped to keep the blood from clotting. After sucking a small amount of blood, the mosquito withdrew, and then prepared to bite the Blue Jay a second time. Before it could do this, the bird flew off and left the mosquito to find more blood elsewhere.

The Blue Jay continued on its way, fulfilling its role as a "bully" among the birds of the bottomland forest. What was not evident at this point, however, was that there was something beginning to grow inside of this bird since its encounter with the mosquito.

The virus inside of the Blue Jay began to incubate and grow. For the first couple of days there were no noticeable effects. Most birds and animals were able to survive after being infected by this particular virus, but this Blue Jay began losing its vision and balance. The virus was affecting its brain functions.

After a couple of more days, the bird was unable to take care of itself. Starving, disoriented and helpless, it dropped from the tree branch it had been resting on, and hit the forest floor with a quiet sound. Disease had taken this individual bird. Before its death, more mosquitoes had fed off of the same Blue Jay. These mosquitoes went on to feed on other animals as well. Those that were susceptible to the effects of the disease met their fates in the same way as the Blue Jay had. Others built up immunities to the disease and continued living. Sometimes these individuals continued to

Cottonwood
By Kevin J. Curtis

be carriers of the virus, even though it no longer affected them.

* * * *

Near the beaver pond, the old cottonwood lay toppled over on the ground. It was rotting and turning into soil. The rich soil of the river valley was filled with organic material from the death and decay of both plants and animals.

Insects and microorganisms helped the process of breaking down the tree into smaller and smaller elements. Almost a century ago, the cottonwood had emerged from a tiny seed that had floated in on the trademark cotton from which these trees derived their name. It had managed to germinate, and over the years, it grew into an enormous tree that had become an important element of the bottomland forest habitat. Now, it had lost its battle with linear time, had grown old, and finally was knocked down by winds and died.

Near the river, the new cottonwood seedling was growing rapidly since the rains had come. Now, as the last warmth of summer was giving in to the chill autumn air, the animals had once again, begun their preparations for the winter season. It seemed that all of the inhabitants of the forest were either eating as much as possible, or they were stockpiling stores of food for winter.

The mouse that lived beneath the old, dead cottonwood tree was hiding seeds inside of its burrow. The rodent had dug down beneath the rotting wood, where it had found both shelter and a natural source of heat. The chemical process of decomposition of the wood produced a small amount of warmth, which was just one of the reasons that the mouse found it such a good place to live.

The Gray Squirrel was burying all sorts of treasures in numerous small holes and cracks and crevices. Most of

Cottonwood
By Kevin J. Curtis

what it was interested in right now were acorns from the oak trees, though it had also buried pine nuts and black walnuts. There was also a lone bitter hickory tree that this squirrel coveted the nuts from.

Flocks of migratory birds were gathering. The marsh was dotted white with egrets, and the trees were filled with blackbirds. Ducks gathered on the river, and they fed and rested up, for the flight south. Hawks and eagles also flew in large numbers to the south, using the rivers to guide them. Many of these raptors would stay, however, until food grew scarce and forced them to move. Great Grey Owls would move from the north if that happened, searching for the voles that made up most of their diet.

After a meal of a small rodent, a Garter Snake wriggled under a rocky ledge, where it would wait out the cold months in hibernation. Some of the animals would sleep during the coldest days, and wake up to search for food when the temperatures warmed. These included raccoons, squirrels, mice and many more. Being larger, the deer had to eat twigs from trees and bushes, as well as the grass and swamp brush that grew tall. These animals might eat five to ten pounds[15] of this fodder each day.

Year-round bird residents such as the Black-capped Chickadee had to eat proportionally large quantities of food to survive. The tiny birds had a high metabolism that required a lot of energy. Such a tiny body was also at risk in severe cold and needed plenty of energy to regulate its body heat. To compensate at night, the chickadee became semi-dormant and its body temperature lowered by several degrees. This adaptation helped to keep it alive during the long winter nights, until it could search for food once morning came.

In the river, marsh and beaver pond, the fish grew less active with the drop in water temperature. Frogs, toads,

Cottonwood
By Kevin J. Curtis

turtles and other amphibians burrowed into the mud to hibernate through the cold winter months. All were preparing for the coming of winter.

As the air temperature continued to fall, the cooling water of the beaver pond began its turnover. As the cold water near the top grew denser and heavier than the warmer water beneath, the water rotated until there was a more consistent temperature throughout the pond. When the temperature dropped below freezing, the marsh and beaver pond developed a layer of ice over the surface. As the temperature continued to drop, the ice grew thicker.

Mounded above the ice, the beavers and muskrats had snug lodges built of mud and sticks. These rodents continued to swim out beneath the ice to find food, such as the stores of branches that the beavers kept below the ice.

As snow fell, it grew deeper and eventually covered the new cottonwood tree that was growing near the river. Dormant now, the tree benefited from the protection of the snow. The white covering held the frozen moisture in and also kept a more steady temperature. The dramatic changes of temperature in the winter, especially if there was a freeze and then thaw from sunny days to frigid nights, was hard on plants. Such action caused the stored water to expand and contract and created stress fractures in the tissues of the plants. Beneath the snow, the cottonwood was insulated from these temperature changes.

When spring arrived in the valley, the sun's rays, now more direct and warming, began to melt the snow pack. As the snow turned to water, it ran into the pond, marsh and river and the banks of these waterways swelled into a spring flood.

Warmer weather meant that the plants would begin to bud and the birds and animals would either return from the south or become more active. As the snow and ice

Cottonwood
By Kevin J. Curtis

disappeared, the residents of the bottomland forest resettled into their summer habitat.

Chapter 16: Outlaws, Robbers and Parasites

When spring settled in, all the forest was alive with plant and animal life. The short growing season in Minnesota was reflected in the speed in which the plants could make use of the warm weather when it arrived. This included the young cottonwood tree. The tree began growing once the soil thawed out, and it seemed to reach up further toward the blue sky each day.

This morning, the heat of the previous day had reacted with the water in the marsh, their temperatures being mismatched at this time of the year. The water was still cold, and the sun's rays beat down during the day raising the temperature of the air and ground. Overnight, a fog had developed and it would take a few hours before the hot sun would burn it off and show the brilliant blue sky.

As a coyote used the dark cover of fog to extend its twilight jaunt, it moved silently along a well-used trail. The wild dog stopped to relieve itself, before returning to the tall grass at the edge of the swamp. The grass was also being used as cover and a launching point for another, much smaller "hunter."

The wood tick, was small, black, and had a tiny design-like marking, on the center of its body. The head was also tiny, which made it perfect for its ability to penetrate the skin of some unsuspecting, warm-blooded creature.

As the coyote trotted past, the wood tick grabbed onto its foreleg and began slowly walking upward. When it rested finally behind the dog's ear, it began the process of attaching itself. First, it used its mouthparts to grab tightly to a piece of skin beneath the shaggy coat of the coyote.

Cottonwood
By Kevin J. Curtis

Then it slowly worked its head deeper into the canine until it was prepared to feed. As it sucked more and more blood out of the animal, the tick grew larger and paler and more hideous–as it grew to enormous proportions in relation to its original size.

The coyote was able to dislodge many of the other ticks, and there were many, with its mouth. This particular one became quite annoying, but it was difficult to reach behind the ear. After it had become quite large and was already backing out and removing its head from inside of the animal's skin, the coyote finally scratched the tick away with its hind leg.

Not far from where the tick landed, a turtle had walked out of the marsh and traveled with much difficulty to the sandy area where it was now busily excavating a hole in the ground. Fairly helpless at this point, the female Painted Turtle continued working with a steady diligence that belied her vulnerability. She did have her shell to hide inside of, but the powerful jaws of a coyote could crack through that shell.

Seemingly unaware of her dangerous situation, or possibly because of it, the turtle deliberately scooped out sand with her legs. When she deemed the hole to be sufficiently deep, she backed further down into it and deposited her eggs, one-by-one. When she finished, she covered the hole back up and slowly, methodically, returned to the water.

Other turtles in the area were doing this exact same thing. It was not unnoticed by the robbers. Later, in the dark of night, a fat raccoon ambled along. Stopping periodically to sniff the night air, it continued on until it found a disturbed patch of ground that smelled of turtle. The raccoon used its small hands to scoop away the dirt and sand until it exposed the nest full of turtle eggs.

Cottonwood
By Kevin J. Curtis

With its black mask over its shiny black eyes, the raccoon was even dressed like a robber as it devoured egg after egg, leaving the leathery shells in a pile around the hole. When it was done, the robber ambled back off into the woods.

Only the fact that the turtles all made their nests about the same time would ensure that a few of them would escape this fate. The sun would warm the ground and incubate the eggs. Once they hatched, the little turtles would have to find their own way to the water. This perilous journey would also take its toll on them, as they could potentially encounter many predators that would enjoy a baby turtle for a meal.

Later in the summer, one of the newly hatched baby turtles was making its way to the beaver pond. It had hatched only hours before, and the tiny turtle had worked long and hard to make it to the water. Nearby, a Great Blue Heron had another baby turtle in its beak. The bird leaned back and swallowed the tiny turtle whole. Completely unaware of the fate of the other turtle, this one slipped into the water and swam past the wading bird as it was occupied with eating.

The heron defecated into the water it was standing in. Inside of its waste, a parasite was beginning a new cycle. Released into the water, the eggs of this parasite would start the process over again.

The *Black Spot Disease* parasite lived inside of the bird's intestines. Later, the eggs hatched in the water, and the larva found a snail to burrow into. Eventually, it produced spores that emerged from the snail and reentered the water.

When the sporocysts[16] came into contact with a Yellow Perch that was living in the pond, they infected the fish and became the black cysts, or spots that lived under its skin and scales. If another bird ate this fish, the cysts would

Cottonwood
By Kevin J. Curtis

mature inside of the intestinal tract of the bird and its eggs would again be passed into the water when the bird defecated.

Such was the life of a parasite. Usually they were rather simple animals, though their lifecycle could be quite complicated and intertwined with several other species. Tapeworms could demonstrate another example of how this might work. Tapeworms could be passed to animals by fleas, after flea larva swallowed the tapeworm eggs.

A parasitic relationship almost always meant that the host animal was being injured in the process. The parasite would take from the host and give nothing in return. Sometimes the host would even die in the end. There were other examples of relationships between species, and some of these were beneficial.

Bees pollinated flowers, which allowed the flower to create a viable seed. In the process, the bee was able to obtain pollen and nectar used for creating food for the bee colony. Each participant benefited from the exchange. This was called a symbiotic relationship. Another example of this would be the bird that ate insects and ticks from the body of an animal such as a cow. The bird got insects to eat, and the cow had ticks or harmful insects removed from its body. Both animals benefited from this symbiotic relationship.

The environment when looked at in its entirety, was a huge intertwined society of plants and animals. Some of these creatures used others for their own benefit, and some used each other to survive. Most often, when a balance was struck between a diverse group of organisms, more of them benefited than not.

When one organism became overpopulated, it affected all the others in the environment. In the case of the river valley, the influx of humans caused the demise of several other species. The human settlers took the land

Cottonwood
By Kevin J. Curtis

away from the native animals and the native people. Their numbers increased so fast, and their interference in the natural environment was so great, that major changes resulted.

* * * *

The cat moved silently, almost motionless except for the rhythmic movement of the tip of her tail. Her stomach was near the ground as she stalked her prey. She had recently had kittens, and her belly sagged from motherhood. The robin hopped along the ground, listening intently with its head cocked to one side. Beneath the soil's surface, the bird could detect the minute sounds of an earthworm.

The bird pounced, beak downward, and began pulling the worm out of the ground. At that precise moment, the cat ran forward and pounced on the bird, killing it with a bite to the back of the head. It was over in a moment and the cat carried her prey back to the shed behind Lyle and Marie's house in Bloomington, Minnesota.

Marie's family had lived in this area for over a hundred years. Her great grandparents, William and Annie Schmidt, had a farm close by, where a neighborhood of houses now stood. Lyle Davidson was originally from Des Moines, and he worked at the airport. Neither Lyle nor Marie knew about the litter of kittens in their shed.

The mother cat brought the bird back into the shed through the crack under the door. The kittens were only a few weeks old, but they were curious about the prize that their mother carried. In the dark of the shed, they cautiously approached the dead robin. Soon they were tugging at the bird and tasting the blood from its wounds. They began stalking it and each other, as the instinct to hunt was awakened.

Cottonwood
By Kevin J. Curtis

Eventually, hunger took over for the mother, and she began crunching through the flesh of the bird as her five kittens nuzzled against her and nursed. These kittens had never had human contact, and they were quickly approaching the age where this lack of human bonding would forever render them wild and thus unfit to be domestic pets.

Feral cats were nothing new. A number of them inhabited this area. The proximity to both the river bottoms and the human habitation proved to be a good situation for them. Most of the large predators were now absent from the woods, while at the same time, food scraps in garbage was common, as well as pet food and bird feeding stations–which made hunting easy. Stored bird food in garages and sheds also attracted mice and other rodents that were suitable prey for these wild cats.

Over the next couple of weeks, the kittens grew larger and stronger. They began wandering off on their own. One of the two males, a large orange colored tabby, was out early one morning when Lyle was leaving for work. Lyle noticed the young cat and approached it when he saw it go into his shed.

When he opened the door of the shed, the orange tabby hissed at him and backed up to the wall. Lyle reached for a broom and went to drive the cat out of the shed. He was surprised when not only did the cat he was pursuing run out, but several more also fled from the shed. Lyle closed the door and went to work.

The orange tabby left the shed, his mother and his siblings. He wandered off the Davidson's property, and down into the river valley along Long Meadow Lake. Once in this bottomland marsh and forest, the orange tabby was soon reluctant to return to the areas inhabited by humans. There were so many things for the young feline to explore and learn about. By instinct and by trial-and-error, he

Cottonwood
By Kevin J. Curtis

would have to either learn to survive on his own, or he would die.

There were plenty of things to eat late in the summer. He satisfied his hunger by eating grasshoppers, frogs, mice and occasionally small snakes or birds. Some of these he had only to happen upon, while others such as songbirds, had to be stalked.

There were also dangers in his new home. Often the areas where he found water to drink were extremely unstable. The mud was deep, and it tried to pull his feet down into it. There were also other animals that were best avoided. Attracted by the smell of food, the orange tabby found a large raccoon eating a fish next to a pool of water. Seeing the cat, the raccoon hissed and charged. The large size of the raccoon made escape the prudent choice and the cat ran away.

On another occasion, a hawk flew down from the sky and attacked the young cat. By some sixth sense, the feline jumped at the last moment and lashed out with his claws before running into the brush. The hawk flew off and made no attempt to pursue. The hawk relied on stealth, and the well-armed cat was capable of causing injury, even if the hawk was able to overpower it.

Once, the orange tabby found itself in a heated battle over territory with a mink. The fight lasted only seconds, before the cat found itself outmatched. It ran away, leaving the civet victorious in this battle. Other animals that the cat learned to avoid were coyotes and the Red Fox. Instinct was correct in telling the orange tabby that a fight with such animals as these could be fatal.

Since the cat often roamed the nighttime, Great Horned Owls also posed a threat. These great birds were truly the masters of the night sky. Since they were quite adept at eating many animals such as rodents and skunks, a

Cottonwood
By Kevin J. Curtis

large owl was probably capable of eating a cat if other prey was in short supply.

As for skunks, the orange tabby had an encounter in a city park with one. Both animals were scavenging the human leftovers in the garbage and around the picnic areas. They were able to ignore each other until they both arrived on the same piece of discarded ham sandwich.

The cat hissed and showed its fangs, whereas the skunk simply turned and "fired." The stink-spray from the skunk sent the cat away with burning eyes, nose and mouth. The smell hung on for weeks, and it was not an encounter that the orange tomcat had any desire to repeat. From that day forward, he stayed clear of skunks, no matter how large or small.

By fall, the orange cat had grown big and strong. He was sufficiently able to take prey and thrived in the river bottoms. He was governed by instinct, some of it hard for humans to understand.

The tomcat sprayed the edges of his territory, to mark it with his scent. He also searched for female cats to impregnate. This drive was so strong, that it brought about a natural, yet abhorrent behavior that was fairly common among cats and some other animals. This was the wanton killing of any kittens that he had not sired.

In most cases, the mother cat would put up a fight, but the difference in size and strength were in his favor. After driving the mother away, he would enter the den or nest, and using his powerful jaws and sharp teeth, he would kill all of the kittens. As horrible as this was by human standards, it usually succeeded in bringing the female back into estrous, at which time he would return to pursue her for mating.

The natural world is difficult, and sometimes cruel. Wild animals don't have "storybook" lives. Domestic animals that turn wild may have it even worse. Human

Cottonwood
By Kevin J. Curtis

intervention in breeding may produce characteristics desired by the human owners, but frequently these same characteristics serve as a disadvantage to the animal in the wilderness. Since cats retained *most* of the characteristics of their wild counterparts, they were better suited to life in the wild than many other animals. Still, a feral cat was no bobcat.

While bobcats were occasionally found in the bottomland forest, the orange tabby was fortunate not to meet one. A bobcat was well adapted to survive in the wild, and a feral (domestic) cat would likely become a meal if it were to meet up with one.

Winter… that season of cruel cold and scarcity, was the taker of life for those who were less-than-fit. This applied to animals both wild and domesticated. For a feral cat, however, winter could be extremely harsh. Softened by their historically long dependence on human beings, the cold and lack of food weighed heavily on the feral cats. Often the winter would send them into human neighborhoods in search of garbage.

The orange tabby had found some shelter from the wind in the valley and had taken up permanent residence inside of the hollow of a fallen tree. He survived by catching mice and voles tunneling just below the surface of the snow. Every now-and-again, he would find some hapless animal or bird that had frozen or starved to death. The hungry cat was not too proud to help himself to carrion when this happened.

By his skill and cunning, and by the fact that he was young and strong, the cat survived the long, dark winters. At the age of four-and-a-half, he was in the prime of his life. By now, he had already sired nearly a hundred offspring, a few who were born to domestic mothers, now resided in suburban homes and apartments. Others were born to mothers who were feral like he was. The mortality

Cottonwood
By Kevin J. Curtis

rate for these kittens was high. If the climate and conditions didn't get them, there were always other male cats willing to kill kittens that were not their own offspring. Not many of these survived long, though a small number may have.

As the warmth of spring set in, the tomcat found plenty to eat again. Life was easier now, except that he was plagued by such parasites as wood ticks, fleas and soon, mosquitoes. There was also an intestinal parasite living inside of him. It was a by-product of the flea infestation, as this parasite was transferred by fleas. It was growing larger and was beginning to affect the cat. The Roundworm was living on the food that the cat consumed. Despite having plenty to eat, the cat began losing weight. The Roundworm larvae infected the cat's lungs, and soon it began to get tired easily.

By midsummer, the orange tabby was skinny and had blood and Roundworm eggs in its feces. The cat's overall health was failing, and with no human intervention, the parasite continued to devastate the animal's internal body functions. If he did survive until winter, it was unlikely that he could survive the cold in his present condition.

His need for more food brought the cat into the human neighborhoods in search of garbage, pet food and whatever he could find. He was nearly hit by a car one day, as he crossed a street to go further into the human occupied territory. His normal cautiousness was being overridden by his insatiable hunger. His brain functions were stressed, like his body, from starvation. Inside his intestines, the parasite continued to grow larger.

A dog attacked him while he was in someone's yard, and he lashed out with his sharp claws. The dog was scratched across his nose and backed away long enough for the cat to flee. The dog continued barking, though it was

Cottonwood
By Kevin J. Curtis

unsure if it wanted to reengage the vicious intruder. The canine's muzzle was now dripping with blood.

    The human neighborhood was dangerous, and the cat quickly made his way back to the woods and down into the river bottoms. He felt safer there. He was tired and panicky from his ordeal. His senses were beginning to fail as starvation took its toll on his mind and body. He ran for the safety of his hollow log.

    Before he made it there, a mother coyote with three half-grown pups saw him and gave chase. The orange tabby turned to run in the opposite direction when he was grabbed by another, larger, male coyote. The teeth of the coyote penetrated the lanky body of the tomcat, and he instinctively lashed out with his claws. The fight ended quickly when the coyote shook the cat in his mouth, and the power of the canine's grip and violent shaking broke the orange tabby's back. With his spine snapped, the cat lost its power to fight back. It lay limp in the coyote's jaws as he trotted off with his prize.

Chapter 17: Management and Preservation

    As the years passed, the young cottonwood tree kept growing quickly. Before too long it had become a sapling with a one inch[5] diameter trunk. In the spring, a mallard hen had decided to make her nest near the tree. Hidden in the tall grass, the nest was little more than a shallow cup of matted plants. The hen continued to lay eggs over the next few days until she had a total of twelve.

    The eggs were white and roughly the size of those that came from a large chicken. The duck sat on the eggs to keep them warm, though she took breaks occasionally to feed or to swim in the river. While there were plenty of nest robbers around, many birds and other ducks were nesting at

Cottonwood
By Kevin J. Curtis

the time and the ducklings were able to hatch. In fact, ten of the original eleven hatched.

When the young ducks were out of their eggshells and finally dried into little brown, downy fluff balls, they ran behind their mother as she waddled down to the river. One by one, the ducklings followed her into the water and with little hesitation, they began swimming behind her.

Scavengers soon discovered the waste left behind in the nest, as the two remaining eggs became rank with rot. The remainder was absorbed into the ground, and so became part of the young cottonwood tree growing there.

Not far away, the U.S. Fish & Wildlife Service staff was working in an area that was being cleared to restore it to the state of Oak Savannah. Fire was the primary force that kept the brush and weeds in check. The sturdy oaks could withstand the fire if it burned through quickly, and only damaged the outer part of the trees.

Humans had worked diligently to prevent or put out fires over the years. Eventually it became apparent that the absence of regular burning, allowed the brush to get out of control. Because of this, work crews cut back the brush and also lit fires in *prescribed burns.* This was one of the conservation tools utilized to revitalize wildlife habitat.

Another method of revitalizing habitat included the construction of levies and water control structures to regulate water levels in the wetlands. Some of this was necessary to compensate for the damage incurred to the environment during the construction of roads, bridges, utilities and other manmade structures.

Public interest in the river valley had instigated the creation of the Minnesota Valley National Wildlife Refuge in 1976. From that point on, the U.S. Fish & Wildlife Service managed this vital habitat.

Funds were now available from the Federal Government to provide for staff and programs to benefit

Cottonwood
By Kevin J. Curtis

both the wildlife in the area, and the people who might use these lands for recreational purposes including, hiking, biking, fishing, berry picking and limited hunting and trapping.

    This refuge became one of only a handful of *urban wildlife refuges* that were in close proximity to major metropolitan areas. In fact, it was among the largest of these urban refuges. With much of the land along the Minnesota River now belonging to the wildlife refuge, it extended some thirty-four miles[17] from the Minneapolis/St. Paul International Airport and (Minnesota's) Fort Snelling State Park, to the cities of Jordan and Carver to the southwest. In addition, the federal lands were adjacent to the state parklands in many areas, which increased the overall size of the wildlife habitat.

    The U.S. Fish & Wildlife Service and the Minnesota Department of Natural Resources worked together to manage these lands. Local police departments also played a role in the law enforcement of these areas that were within their various jurisdictions. Also involved was the *Friends of the Minnesota Valley* organization that came into being in 1982.

    With the vast area of land encompassed by the wildlife refuge, the paid staff could not do all of the work necessary to adequately manage it. Because of this, volunteers became an important part of the team. Volunteer staff helped with programs, interpretive hikes, species counts, eradication of invasive plant species and also by providing valuable information about what was happening in and around the wildlife refuge.

    The visitor center for the refuge was somewhat unique, compared to many of the others around the country. It had a theater; a museum, a gift shop and a beautiful overlook just outside. Visitors were also able to watch as a huge variety of wild birds visited the feeding stations that

Cottonwood
By Kevin J. Curtis

were situated in view of the large windows of the center. Programs for children and school groups ran frequently. There were also interpretive programs for adults that included hikes within the different sections, or *units* of the refuge.

Unfortunately, not everything that went on in the wildlife refuge was either good or even legal. Dumping of garbage continued as well as other misuses. People did not heed signs that prohibited dogs from being unleashed. In the national wildlife refuge, it was considered that the tiniest mouse had more right to be there than an unleashed dog or a person. Still, some dogs were let loose, to the detriment of the wildlife.

A few places in the wildlife refuge were closed. Some of them were closed for part of the breeding season to prevent the disturbance of certain species of birds, such as the heron colony in west Wilkie. Certain areas had to be closed because they were becoming meeting places for men with *alternative lifestyles.* This activity made it undesirable for others to visit, especially with children.

Another rule prohibited anyone from being in the wildlife refuge after dark, except with permission from the park staff. Much of the nighttime activity included illegal parties that generated leftover trash. Beer and liquor bottles, and cans along with plastic bags and food wrappers, were often discarded at these sites. Frequently, these parties also had illegal fires.

Sometimes the secluded areas of the refuge provided the environment for more sinister activities, such as the killing of an unwanted domestic animal. Sometimes the dead bodies that were found there were people.

In November of 1993, a federal officer found a car in one of the refuge parking lots. He approached the car, and through the window he could see the bodies of two people slumped over. Blood was splattered inside and

Cottonwood
By Kevin J. Curtis

against the windows. This looked like a crime scene, so he called the local police.

What the officer had discovered inside of the car, was the body of a fifteen-year-old teenage boy who had been missing, along with his thirty-year-old neighbor, who had been accused of molesting him. Inside of the car there was a gun, and both bodies had bullet wounds. It was thought to be perhaps, a murder and suicide, though what really happened, no one was completely sure.

Most of the illegal activity was more minor in nature, however. Some of it involved breaking hunting or fishing regulations, or on occasion, the arson of a fishing pier. Much of what occurred was beyond the view of the limited staff that was available to manage these things.

* * * *

The truck circled the parking lot before it finally came to a stop. The driver wanted to be sure that no one else was around. He cautiously got out, and then opened the back of the truck.

In back, there were two beautiful puppies. The female was a thin animal, colored black and white with long hair and a pointed muzzle. The male looked like a beagle mix, and was brown and white. Each looked as if it had recently been wearing a collar, though neither was wearing one now. Once they jumped out of the truck, they began to wag their tails and explore the area. The two were obviously used to being together, and they followed each other, with the beagle mix being the more adventurous of the two.

The man grabbed a bag of dog food, and carried it to the trailhead. Just through the gate, he poured a bunch of kibble onto a manhole cover near the drainage pond. The two puppies were hungry, and they began to eat as the man

Cottonwood
By Kevin J. Curtis

walked back to the truck and drove off before they noticed he had gone.

Eventually, the two puppies had eaten enough so that they noticed that the man who brought them was no longer in sight. They also were intrigued by the water, woods and all of the new sounds and smells. They began to wander around, though they didn't venture too far from the trailhead where they were abandoned.

A volunteer ranger was just beginning his hike on the Bluff Trail, when he noticed that someone had poured a heaping pile of dog food on a manhole cover at the trailhead where the drainage pond was diverted into Long Meadow Lake. His first thought was that "some idiot was feeding the animals again."

People, who thought that they were being helpful, often fed the wild animals in the wildlife refuge. Such activities had increased the presence of such nuisance creatures as raccoons, deer and squirrels that often came into nearby yards, gardens and garbage cans and pillaged when such leftovers ran out. Of course there were also the "bread people." These were the people who thought that large quantities of processed bread products were good for ducks and other wildlife. In reality, most animals had difficulty digesting bread, and it sometimes turned into fatal blockages in these birds' and animals' digestive systems.

Thinking that there was little he could do about the dog food dump, the volunteer continued on with his hike. After a few hours, he returned to the trailhead to find two puppies that greeted him enthusiastically. That was when the volunteer ranger put the day's events into order.

The dog food had not been left for the wild animals. It was left for the two puppies that someone had abandoned! He was perplexed and angry. Why would someone abandon these two beautiful puppies when there

Cottonwood
By Kevin J. Curtis

were animal shelters that would take them? This was simply cruel to let such young, unguarded dogs loose here to fend for themselves. Quite possibly, if left overnight, they might end up as food for the local coyotes.

Had he a different living situation, the ranger would have taken the dogs home with him. Instead, he called on his cell phone to the law enforcement officer of the Minnesota Valley National Wildlife Refuge. The officer answered, but informed the ranger that he was at a game fair in Anoka County. He was quite a distance away. He did say that he would contact the Bloomington police and have an animal control officer pickup the two strays.

The volunteer decided to wait with the two puppies. The male was getting rambunctious and wanted to run into the woods. The female was reluctant to either let her friend out of her sight, or to leave the kind human who was stroking her long black fur. Eventually, another kindhearted hiker stopped to help "baby-sit" the two puppies, while waiting for the animal control officer.

Eventually, after a long wait, a regular police squad came into the parking lot of the Old Cedar Bridge. The volunteer ranger flagged down the officer and asked if he was there for the puppies. The officer had no knowledge of the situation and was just on a routine patrol. He radioed to see if anyone else was coming for the dogs and found out that no one was.

The two puppies were coaxed into the back of the squad car and the police officer reassured the two good Samaritans that the puppies would be held for ten days and then offered for adoption. Such beautiful, young puppies stood an excellent chance of finding good homes, he said.

The volunteer ranger watched as the police car drove off with the two dogs in the backseat. Then, he got into his own car and drove home.

Cottonwood
By Kevin J. Curtis

Chapter 18: Historical Leftovers

One of the interesting things about the land in the Minnesota Valley National Wildlife Refuge was the bits of leftover history that remained. Some were barely noticeable, like the remnants of foundations or farm equipment that might be found during an off-trail hike. Others were noticeable, and would almost "stare" back at you when you found them. These included the old Jab's Farm site and Ehmiller (though much of this was demolished in 2005 for safety) farm site at Louisville Swamp.

Among the historic treasures within the refuge were the old Bass Ponds located close to the airport and Mall of America in Bloomington. Due to intensive fishing pressure, Largemouth Bass were disappearing from many lakes around Minneapolis in the early 1900's. Judson L. Wicks, who was the president of the (Minneapolis chapter of the) Izaak Walton League at the time, found a location east of Cedar Avenue in the Minnesota River bottoms. The creek was spring-fed, and provided the water for a series of manmade ponds. The site was leased in 1926 to produce game fish to stock in Minnesota lakes. The Minnesota State Game and Fish department and U.S. Department of Fisheries provided assistance to the Bass Ponds project over the thirty-plus years it was in operation.

In 1938, Dr. Samuel Eddy, from the University of Minnesota used the Bass Ponds to experiment with creating hybrids of Muskellunge and Northern Pike. These fish ate tremendous quantities of minnows (and salamanders), and they would eat each other when the food ran out.

Upstream from the ponds, native Brook Trout lived in the cold, clean water of the creek that supplied water to the ponds. The ponds were manmade, and the newer ones

Cottonwood
By Kevin J. Curtis

were created by the Works Projects Administration. These were dug by crews of men with shovels and wheelbarrows.

Wood Duck houses were put up, and the Long Meadow Lake area was an excellent duck hunting location. In fact, during the blizzard on November 11, 1940, some hunters were trapped in the pass for two weeks. Some of them froze to death.

Gill netting on Long Meadow Lake also provided carp for the cannery. Other fish that were raised in the Bass Ponds included, sunfish, Black Crappies, Smallmouth Bass, Northern Pike, Grayling, Walleyes and Golden Shiners. Unfortunately, The Izaak Walton League lost their lease after intense pressure to develop around the area.

By the 1960's, a gravel mining operation that excavated parts of the southwestern ridge, contributed to the decline and pollution of the area. When the Minnesota Valley National Wildlife Refuge took over in 1976, staff began restoring the Bass Ponds to their original state. The area then became an educational and recreational area.

Just north of the Bass Ponds, the last farm remained, in spite of the construction of the Minneapolis/St. Paul International Airport, the Mall of America, business such as Cypress Semiconductor, numerous roads, single-family homes and apartment buildings. This one farm survived in spite of efforts to remove it to put the land to "better use." Well after the Mall of America and Light Rail Transit system were built, one could still see sheep and lamas at this farm.

Along the Bluff Trail in the Minnesota Valley National Wildlife Refuge, there were places where Christian missionary, Gideon Pond and Dakota (Sioux) Chief Cloud Man found water and building materials. Both settled in Oak Grove (in Bloomington, MN).
Cloud Man's village, Reyataotonwe (Inland Village), was originally located west of Mde Maka Ska (White Earth

Cottonwood
By Kevin J. Curtis

Lake), which would later be known as Lake Calhoun. It was there that Philander Prescott began teaching Cloud Man's village to use a plow and farm the land.

Cloud Man moved his tribe to Oak Grove (Bloomington) in 1839, because of a renewed conflict with the Ojibwe. Gideon Pond and his brother Samuel were trying to teach the indigenous people about farming, while simultaneously attempting to convert them to Christianity. The Dakota mission was first located at the site in 1843.

After the Dakota people were moved to a reservation further up the Minnesota River in 1852, Gideon Pond purchased the land and built a house there in 1856. The house was later turned into an interpretive museum by the City of Bloomington.

The area had a long history, with the Dakota Mdewakanton (Sioux) being the primary American Indian tribe. The other major tribe in this area was the Ojibwe. Because of a long history of intertribal warfare, the U.S. Government decided it would be necessary to split the two tribes geographically. In 1825, it was agreed by the Dakota and Ojibwe that the Dakota would live south of the Minnesota River, and the Ojibwe would live on the north side of the river.

This was not the first time that white people influenced this part of Minnesota. In the late 1600's, Father Louis Hennepin, Daniel Greysolon and Sieur Du Luth had visited the area that would later become Minneapolis. An explorer named Jonathan Carver spent the winter in Chief Shakopee's village in 1766, and he engaged the Dakota people in trade.

Zebulon Pike came to the area in 1805, on a mission to find land to build a fort. The rivers were the main means of travel in those days, and he camped on an island where the Minnesota and Mississippi rivers met (This area was called, "Mdote Minisota," and was considered to be the

Cottonwood
By Kevin J. Curtis

center of the world by the Dakota people). Later, this island would be called Pike Island, and it would have the more sinister history, of being a concentration camp for American Indians being held by the U.S. Government.

Prior to that, Pike spent time with Little Crow and his Dakota band. The fort that was built nearby was named Fort Snelling, after Colonel Josiah Snelling, who headed the effort of building the fort.

Also worth noting in this area, was Camp Coldwater. This land located around a natural spring was significant in many ways. For over ten thousand years, Native Americans had used this place as a peace site. It was, and still is a sacred place for the American Indians. It was also the place where the soldiers camped from 1820 to 1822, while Fort Snelling was being built.

Unfortunately, the sacred spring was threatened later, by construction of a highway system, and it became the property of the U.S. Federal Bureau of Mines. Access was severely limited by a gate that was kept locked except for regular business days, during regular day hours. The sacred oak trees were also felled, and the American Indians and others protested to save the sacred spring from complete destruction.

Other Dakota villages in the region (during the first half of the nineteenth century), included Little Crow's in what is now South St. Paul, and Black Dog's, which was located where the power plant would later stand. Pennesha's village was located (in Bloomington) near the mouth of Nine Mile Creek (so named because it was nine miles from Fort Snelling). Chief Shakopee's village stood where the city of Shakopee would later be located. Though the river now separated the Dakota and Ojibwe, their problems had not gone away.

Both tribes had suffered from the loss of game animals such as bison, moose, elk and bear. Diseases such

Cottonwood
By Kevin J. Curtis

as Whooping Cough also decimated the Indian population. As food grew scarce, alcoholism spread and diseases took their toll, the Native Americans were forced to make a very difficult decision. Eventually, the Ojibwe and Dakota people found it necessary to sell their ancestral lands in order to draw rations from the U.S. Government. This was the final step that pushed the American Indians out of the area and opened it up for European (and other) settlers.

As time continued on, changes occurred rapidly. As one chapter unfolded in the development instigated by the new human inhabitants, that which had preceded, was left behind. Sometimes these "leftovers" remained as old foundations, discarded materials or simply as memories.

One such historical leftover was the Bloomington Ferry. The first, permanent white settlers in the area were Peter Quinn and his wife, who came in 1843. Eventually, a means to cross the Minnesota River was needed, so that people had a way to get to Shakopee and Mankato to the south. William Chambers and Joseph Dean came in 1849, to run the Bloomington Ferry. The ferry shuttled people and goods from one side of the river to the other, and operated until the building of the Bloomington Ferry Bridge in 1889 (which put the ferry out of business). Later the name Bloomington Ferry would be applied to one of the units of the Minnesota Valley National Wildlife Refuge.

Perhaps one of the most controversial leftovers came from the original human inhabitants of the area. Some of the burial mounds went all the way back to prehistoric times. Continued development threatened the final resting places of these American Indian forebears. The burial mounds were not always easy to distinguish. There were no grave markers like the white people used. Still, many of these burial sites were known for over a hundred years before they became the focal point of heated legal battles.

Copyright © 2008 by Kevin J. Curtis

Cottonwood
By Kevin J. Curtis

While the burial sites were sacred to the American Indians, others had raided these sites over the years to retrieve artifacts. The tools, jewelry and clothing buried with the deceased, proved irresistible to some who would later desecrate these graves.

There were originally thirty-six mounds found in what would later become Mounds Spring Park (by Indian Mounds Elementary school) in Bloomington. By the end of the twentieth century, only twenty could still be found. Near 34th Avenue and Old Shakopee Road, another site called Lincoln Mound 2, was threatened by development.

The area east of the Mall of America was under intense pressure for development, and this is where these burial mounds were located. Minnesota state law, Section 8 of MS 307.08 (passed in 1979), provided for the protection and acquisition of large Indian cemeteries. It did not, however, define what constituted a "large cemetery," or what government department was responsible for acquiring and protecting such a site. This ambiguity opened the door for strained relationships between those concerned with respecting the remains of the deceased, and those who were pushing the development of the Minnesota Valley, bluff top lands.

Furthermore, while the state Minnesota Indian Affairs Council took such issues on a case-by-case basis, it seemed that generally, a few burial mounds, like perhaps less than ten, did not suffice to be seen as a site worthy of the same protections as a "large" cemetery.

At one point, protesters camped at the site of Lincoln Mound 2, thus preventing the heavy equipment from digging up the land, and so disturbing the graves. Police were also at the site trying to keep order, and trying to keep people from trespassing.

The situation was emotionally charged, and protesters became more belligerent. The resulting police

Cottonwood
By Kevin J. Curtis

actions were declared "brutality" by those protesting. At one point, a protester heard a gunshot, and found two officers had shot his dog that was tied outside of his trailer. The police officers said the dog had attacked, but it was said to have been a docile animal and police killed it out of retribution.

During excavation, the first human remains were found on July 23, 2004. The decision had been made by the Minnesota Indian Affairs Council, to remove the remains and put them in the Bluff Ridge Mound (created by the Ceridian Corporation when mounds were moved to construct that building) across the road. In retrospect, it appears that politics had played a role in the process, since it was possible to revise the plans for development enough to avoid disturbing the gravesite.

Much of the political and legal battle took place behind closed doors and the particulars were forever lost. Speculations were made as to why the Minnesota Indian Affairs Council, which was made up of American Indians, did not fight harder to protect these mounds. Some speculated that it had to do with non-Indian groups pushing for state-run casinos. Forcing the issue of protecting a sacred site near the Mall of America, might harm the interests of the two Dakota-run casinos located south of the Twin Cities. Others wondered if it was because the Minnesota Indian Affairs Council had more Ojibwe members, and the mounds were in (Dakota) Sioux territory.

Truthfully, the mounds may have been there so long that they even predated the occupation of the Dakota people. Archeological evidence points to the Dakota having been preceded by two or three other cultures in the Minnesota River Valley, over some 12,000 years of Paleo-Indian culture. In the middle 1600's, the Dakota replaced the Oneota and Iowa tribes. It is possible that the graves found were ancient. The Minnesota Indian Affairs Council

Cottonwood
By Kevin J. Curtis

gave limited information, and archaeologists were frequently caught between the struggling factions and not always allowed to do tests that would determine such things.

In the case of Lincoln Mound 2, no photographs were allowed. Drawings made of the remains were shredded prior to internment in the Bluff Ridge Mound.

The organization that was most involved in trying to preserve the burial mounds was the Mendota Mdewakanton Dakota Community (MMDC), which was a non-federally recognized Native American group. Perhaps it was simply because this organization had less political reason to avoid the issue explains why it was more active in preserving the integrity of the burial mounds than the federally recognized tribes were.

While Lincoln Mound 2 created intrigue and controversy, it was certainly not the only burial site in the Minnesota River Valley. There were in fact, as many as 1,000 surveyed in the Twin Cities, Metropolitan area. This number grew to around 10,000 statewide. Undoubtedly, there are numerous others, yet undiscovered or perhaps destroyed by development or erosion. Some prehistoric sites may have nearly completely disintegrated by the time major development began in the area.

Many of the surveyed sites were located on private land. There were also areas within public land, including the Minnesota Valley National Wildlife Refuge. These burial mounds, some ancient, were a reminder that others had lived in the area for thousands of years. These past cultures had done little to change or damage the land, water and air, and yet, the drive toward industrialization had damaged, destroyed or changed so much of the little bit that these people had left behind.

During the 1960's, excavations of Indian burial mounds were for "research" purposes. The remains found

Cottonwood
By Kevin J. Curtis

were usually analyzed and sent to museums–sometimes even put on display. It wasn't until 1971, when this practiced stopped.

The State of Minnesota enacted a private cemeteries law that made it a crime to disturb human remains that were buried on either public or private lands. This law put an end to the excavation of gravesites for research purposes, and put greater restrictions on how old gravesites were treated in regard to development.

It was largely the changes in public opinion that fueled the creation of the laws that were enacted. No longer were burial mounds simply something to be exploited or an inconvenience to progress and development. They were the remains of someone's loved ones.

Chapter 19: The "Life" of a Burial

He was running. Horses had not yet arrived on the continent, as the Spanish had yet to travel to the "new world." His people *would* have a great horse culture, but that was far off in the future. At this point in time, as he ran through the valley, there were three basic means of transportation. You could walk, run, or paddle a canoe. The river that flowed through the great river valley was the "highway" of the time. The river valley itself and the surrounding area had been home to his people "forever."

At eleven winters of age, he had already survived many hardships. He was nearing manhood, and even now, he had great responsibility. He was relaying a message to his uncle who lived two-day's run from his father's village. There was danger from an enemy tribe, and his village needed help.

Such tribal warfare was an unfortunate condition of the indigenous people who lived here. It was also a necessity in a culture that held the ways of the warrior in

Cottonwood
By Kevin J. Curtis

high esteem. The boy was already skilled in using the spear, club, axe and atlatl.[18] He traveled light now, as speed was of the utmost importance.

He was sparsely clothed, as the temperature was moderate and his cross-country run caused his body to generate plenty of heat. An expert at foraging for food, the boy had accompanied his mother as a small child when she gathered plants, roots and berries for the family. Later, he graduated from this "woman's work," to hunting small game such as beavers, rabbits and birds. Eventually, his father honored him, by inviting his son to join in the hunting of deer, elk and bison.

These large animals were best captured, by chasing them into a bog or the deep mud in the swampy areas of the river valley. Once the animal became encumbered by the muck and mud, the men ran forward and used spears to kill it.

The boy's mind was busily thinking about these things as he ran. When his mind was otherwise occupied, he did not focus on how tired he was or the flies and mosquitoes that were pursuing him. Sweat ran down his back, and his long black hair was stringy from the combination of sweat and wind. His feet were bare, and the soles were worn into a hardened, leather-like consistency.

He was on the return trip to his village. He had left the village of his uncle the day before, and had slept only a few hours when it became too dark to run. Night also brought out dangers. Lions, bears and wolves were abundant in his world, and these animals were not as wary of man at this early point in history. Such wariness would result after centuries of contact between these animals and the continuously better-armed human beings that lived here.

When he did sleep, the boy had sought the refuge of a small cottonwood tree. The tree was sturdy enough to

Cottonwood
By Kevin J. Curtis

support him, yet small enough to allow the agile young man to climb into it. Once situated in the limbs of the tree, the boy knew that he was better able to defend himself from attack, by using his spear on any lion or bear that might try to climb up after him. The tree was also large enough so that it would be difficult, even for a powerful bear to push down.

At the first light of morning, the boy dropped quietly from his perch. Taking only enough time to urinate, he continued to run–eventually finding that pace that both ate the distance, and came so naturally that he could hold onto it for hours or even days.

By the time the midday heat began, he was entering familiar territory. Though by now he had been running for most of the last four days, he swam the width of the river without much difficulty. The current was strong, and he was pulled along so that he was a considerable distance downriver from where he had started on the other side. When he reached the far bank, he pulled himself from the water. He climbed the steep, mud-slicked bank and sat on the top, puffing as he tried to catch his breathe. Looking down at his leg, the boy found the source of the strange sensation he felt upon emerging from the river. It was a leech, and it had attached itself by its mouth to his skin. He pulled it loose and threw it onto dry land to die.

His physical conditioning was such, that in more modern times, he would be the equivalent of a world-class athlete. After his breathing stabilized, He picked up his spear with its Clovis point, and continued on the last leg of his journey.

First to meet him, were the dogs. Most recognized him as a resident of the village, though one decided to give in to its predatory instinct to give chase. Ironically, when the boy turned and slammed the shaft of his spear across its head, the animal exhibited the counterpoint to that

Cottonwood
By Kevin J. Curtis

behavior, which was to run from that which was chasing you.

As he entered the village, the boy realized that something was wrong. The usual activities associated with life in the village were absent. Present, were the sobering sounds of sorrow and of death. Unaware of his own exhaustion, the boy wandered into the village and to his father's summer dwelling. No one was there, so he continued on to his grandfather's dwelling.

That was where he found his parents and sister. They welcomed him back soberly, and informed him of the death of his grandfather. Had they not told him, the wailing of his grandmother would have given him a good indication of what had happened. She was in an inconsolable, nearly hysterical state.

By tradition, the wife of a recently deceased warrior went through a rather intense ritual of mourning. She was wild-looking. She had not eaten or drank any water for two days since her husband's death. She had not bathed, changed clothes or slept. Her hair was tangled and dirty. Her clothing and skin was marred by dirt and dried blood from her self-mutilation. She had used a knife to cut her arms and legs.

The image was both distressful and frightening for the boy, though he had seen this ritual enacted many times before in his young life. Simultaneously he was distraught over his grandmother's current condition, and the realization of the loss of his grandfather, whom the boy had held in extremely high esteem.

The next day, men from his uncle's village arrived to take up arms against the enemies who were threatening the boy's village. It was these same enemies who had killed his grandfather in a raid that occurred in the night while the boy was gone delivering his message. Preparations were now being made for both a funeral ceremony, and for a

Cottonwood
By Kevin J. Curtis

retaliatory raid against those who had attacked the village and killed a respected elder.

His grandfather's life had been ended by a single blow to the head with a hand axe. The result was both deadly and ghastly, as it had opened the skull and blood and brain tissue had poured out. The body was now wrapped, but decay was quick in the summer months, and the smell was already noticeable and flies were congregating in the area. It was paramount that the burial should take place as soon as possible.

Normally, it was customary in this tribe to place the body on a platform or tie it high in a tree. After the normal process of decay and being scavenged by birds and small creatures, the bones were removed and placed in, and normally above, a preexisting mound in a *secondary burial,* where others had been buried before. During winter, the frozen ground generally prevented any other type of burial. This was not the case now, however, as it was summer. This process of using a secondary burial was dismissed under the current circumstances, due to the risk of immanent attack by enemies of the tribe. Such a burial would allow the body to be exposed during an attack. Because of this, a *primary burial* was used, so that the body would be placed whole, into the ground.

They carried the deceased to the land where their dead ancestors were laid to rest. Their spiritual leader, an elder, designated the exact location. Without writing, knowledge was passed down orally, and among the duties of the spiritual leader, was to remember where burials were located and to decide where new ones should be placed.

Since there were no actual grave markers, it was not unheard of, that the bones of another might accidentally be unearthed during a burial ceremony. In such a situation, these bones were simply (and carefully) replaced. There was much wailing done by those closest to the fallen man,

Cottonwood
By Kevin J. Curtis

and a feast was given, to honor the dead. Both the new dead, and those from long ago were honored, and asked to guide the living through the trials and tribulations yet to come. A woodland bison had been killed to provide meat. The dead man was buried with his few possessions. These included an axe and knife, to be used in the afterlife. The body was placed in an upright position, with the knees drawn up and the head resting on them.

The boy's face and body was painted, as were others in the village. They had used colors obtained from plants and soil to create patterns on their skin that would serve as both a sign of respect for the dead, and also to wear when they went into battle against their enemies. This impending battle was forefront at the moment, and caused the participants to be on guard during the funeral ceremony–which was slightly abbreviated for this reason.

Before and after the soil was carefully mounded up around the body, the spiritual leader chanted and smudged[19] the area and all those present. Then, the people of the village filed away, except for the widow. The boy looked back once, to see his grandmother sobbing, stooped over the burial mound that contained her dead husband. She collapsed on the ground in her sorrow.

The boy looked away and followed his father back to the village. Later, he would follow his father into battle in a blood feud that was older than he was. He would either show himself to be a true warrior, or he would follow his grandfather into the next life. This he knew for sure, though he did not know what hardship the next day would bring.

Cottonwood
By Kevin J. Curtis

Chapter 20: The "Future" of a Burial Mound

It was the 1950's. Development was growing everywhere, including in the areas around the Minnesota River Valley. As the bluff tops were excavated, bones were sometimes unearthed. There were no strict rules regarding such finds, and many had actually been unearthed and scavenged long ago.

On some occasions, archeologists were brought in to excavate the remains of these past residents of the river valley. At that time, this usually meant that the remains would be dug up, and removed to museums where they may or may not be placed on display. Other times, the bones were simply pushed aside, so that they would not complicate the matters of digging and building on the site.

* * * *

It was the summer of 1883. The two boys had finished their chores. School at the one-room school house was out for the summer. They had fished some, and while looking for something else to do, they began digging a hole.

The hole was next to the plowed field where the crops were knee-high. Just at the edge of the field was a small mound of earth that seemed as good a spot as any for them to dig. Part of the mound had been cut away by the plow, and there had been some old bones and Indian arrowheads found around that part of the field.

No one had found any arrowheads for quite awhile, but the two boys soon discovered more bones and arrowheads when they dug into the mound. Excited, they continued digging, until they had unearthed a few relics and they stood dirty, and dripping with sweat–grinning from ear to ear.

Cottonwood
By Kevin J. Curtis

* * * *

Late in the summer of 1958, archeologists from the University were actively surveying and digging in a suspected Indian burial mound. They dug through the soil, and created another similar mound behind them as they worked. Some of the bones were reburied in this new mound, but others were kept, along with other artifacts. These would later be labeled and kept in the basement of a museum.

There were no particular rules regarding the unearthing of these old burial sites. These archeologists considered their work to be valuable research. They were "preserving" the artifacts, by digging them up and removing them for safe storage at a museum.

This was also a time in United States history, when American Indians had fewer rights and protections by law. It would be two more decades before the American Indian Religious Freedom Act of 1978. It was a time when the burial sites of Native Americans were not protected, and they were often desecrated in the name of "research and progress."

* * * *

It was early in the twenty-first century. Available, undeveloped land in the Twin cities, Metropolitan Area was running low. The pressure to develop brought an interesting situation, as developers were forced to change their policies and practices in the new climate of public opinion, and legal procedures.

With the knowledge that Indian burial mounds were likely located on the property slated for construction, the developer hired a private archeological firm to expedite the process legally required by the state of Minnesota, regarding the preservation of private cemeteries. The state archeologist would still need to "signoff," on the project,

Cottonwood
By Kevin J. Curtis

but it was well worth the money spent, to pay a private company and avoid any long delays. If remains were found, and if they were Indian, the Minnesota Indian Affairs Council would need to be consulted as to how to proceed.

  The project was still in the planning stages, but significant excavation was being considered for the areas in question. The archeology team began working on the area, and soon found that there were indeed, several mounds in the area with remains. It was also noted, that some of these had already been damaged or destroyed by crop production and perhaps by earlier excavations.

  The remains found, were indeed thought to be of American Indian origins. The details of the findings were not made public, in compliance with the wishes of the Minnesota Indian Affairs Council. At this point, revisions were made to the design plan of the building and grounds. Efforts were made to work around the undisturbed burial mounds. Those that were disturbed would be removed and reburied nearby. A ceremony would be performed by members of a local Indian tribe, in conjunction with the reburial. Access would also be provided for spiritual ceremonies at the site, once the construction was completed.

* * * *

  The roar of a chainsaw could be heard, and the sound of a limb shredder and heavy equipment. A crew wearing hardhats was busily dismantling an old cottonwood tree that had stood on the site for almost a century. It had once been home to eagles, and had witnessed many changes over the years. Now this particular tree was blocking progress, and it was paying the ultimate price for that.

  Survey markers were visible across the property, parceling off areas that were slated for one thing or the

Cottonwood
By Kevin J. Curtis

other. All was being made ready for the pilings and foundations. There was, however, one little problem that had yet to be sorted out. There was an old set of burial mounds on the other side of the property.

Years ago, such a thing would have likely been handled with bulldozers, and little regard for the dead of long ago. These were different times now, as minority and special interest groups gained legal power and public opinion changed from a mentality of pillaging the land, to one of respecting others, even those who had died long ago.

On that "problem" side of the property, a team of archeologists gently brushed the soil away from the bone fragments. This burial mound had, so it seemed, been disturbed over the years. Perhaps more accurately, it had been destroyed. There were still bones and bone fragments found during the dig, along with a stone axe.

"These bones are likely ancient," said the man delicately brushing away the soil. He put his head down closer to the find.

"This is remarkable!" he said. "This looks like part of the cranium." There are cracks throughout, but some look older than the others."

"Could it have been damaged on more than one occasion?" asked his colleague.

"Possibly, but likely some of these fractures occurred at the time of death," said the first man. "This individual may have been killed, rather than to have died of natural causes."

"Too bad we can't take the bones back for research," said the second man.

The fact was, they would not be allowed to take the bones back to their laboratory for further investigation. This was, of course, exactly what an archeologist would be inclined to do. There were, however, other factors involved in this project that would prevent this from happening.

Cottonwood
By Kevin J. Curtis

First, was the fact that they were merely working to insure that the developer was in compliance with the laws regarding building on or near sites with human remains. This did not necessitate the need to do a forensic study of what may have caused the death of the individual whose bones they were. Further study would not be funded by the developer, as it was not within the sphere of interest regarding this project.

Second, the Minnesota Indian Affairs Council would not allow such activities. Photography of the site and bones was not allowed by the council, and drawings were to be destroyed at the time of reburial. There would be no research conducted. Respect for the dead was of paramount interest to the Indians.

"It always makes me wonder," said the first man, "what happened, who the person was, how he or she died, how they lived…"

"I guess that's why we got into this business huh?" asked the second man.

"Yes, it is," replied the first man. "It's only too bad that money and politics run the show now. Think of what we could learn here."

"Not too loud!" said the second man, "here comes the boss with the Indian representatives."

Their boss was all about business, and she approached the two archeologists. Beside her, were two large American Indian men, wearing their hair in long, ponytails. Coming quickly toward the worksite, were two others, a man and a woman both dressed in business suits.

The first woman owned the archeological firm. She had advanced degrees and was well qualified in the field. She had given up "playing in the dirt," long ago, and was now more of a businessperson, out to make money. She had lost the curiosity and passion for the work that her two employees still had. This project to her, was about

Cottonwood
By Kevin J. Curtis

compliance with the law. That was how she earned her money. She kept her clients' land interests at the forefront of every project. The two American Indian men with her were representatives of the Minnesota Indian Affairs Council.

"Here they come now," the boss lady said to the two Indian men, "I'll make sure that my people handle this exactly the way you wish."

The Indians nodded, and when the man and woman in business suits arrived, the boss lady introduced them all. The Indians sat down near to where the two archeologists were still working. They began unrolling a cloth, and inside, there was a prayer pipe and tobacco.

The boss lady walked off with the two individuals in the suits.

"My people can handle this," she said. "We'll satisfy the Indians and the state, and get you what you need to begin construction."

"Keep me informed of the progress," said the man. "We want to start 'breaking ground' as soon as possible."

"If there are any legal difficulties," said the woman in the suit, "I'm available. Just call my office and someone will be straight out."

The woman in the suit handed business cards to the other two, and walked back to her car. The boss lady and man spoke for a few more minutes before doing the same.

Near the work-site, the two American Indian men passed their pipe back and forth. They were in no hurry to leave, which put an added sense of stress on the two archeologists. As for the archeologists, they continued to do the work that made them money, and brushed aside the desire to find out more about the details of the individual who was buried there–just as they brushed away the soil from the bones.

Cottonwood
By Kevin J. Curtis

"Don't lose that soil," called out one of the Indians. "That soil is the bodies of our ancestors."

The archeologists nodded back, because in this statement, they could only find truth. For in that very soil, were the last remains of a man who had died very long ago from a blow to the head by a hand-axe, much like the one his bones had been found with. And though his immediate family members were gone now too, some of them perhaps buried nearby, he had been a person much cared about in life.

Chapter 21: Anatomy of an Accident

The road cut through the river valley and wound along the Minnesota River. It was not a busy road, yet the two-lane blacktop had its share of traffic. Not so long before, this area had been undivided by such things as roads. The woods, meadows and marshes still lined this stretch of pavement in many places for miles at a time. To the north, the river ran parallel to the road. On the east end near the state parkland, the road went between the river and the lake. On the east end of the lake was the power plant.

Periodically, one might be lucky enough to see a line of ducklings following their mother along the side of the road. If a person was very observant, he or she might even notice the young Wild Turkeys following their mother, each one a miniature version of the adult. In short, though human development was encroaching into the area, plenty of wildlife still inhabited these undeveloped areas.

The speed limit was posted, though most of the cars that came through were traveling much faster. There didn't seem to be any real need to go slow here. The road was not busy, though it got quite dark after the sun went down.

David was roaring down this stretch of road one evening just at dusk. The moon was in view just above the

Cottonwood
By Kevin J. Curtis

horizon, and looked as if it was a gigantic, orange globe. The car was new, a Mazda RX7, and the temptation was high to push the limits and see how fast he could go down the straight stretch that ran parallel to the river.

He had driven this stretch everyday for over a year now, and though he had seen police cars on occasion, it was usually not patrolled. He pressed down on the accelerator and the car shot forward as Dave shifted the manual five-speed transmission and increased his speed. His intent was to make a short burst of speed and then coast down before he reached the far end of the road. Out here in the middle, there was nothing but a straight piece of road with nobody around; or so he thought.

The thrill of the drive was evident in his face as Dave roared across the asphalt, with the windows down and the wind rushing through the car. His hair whipped wildly in the late summer evening, as the whine of the Mazda's engine filled the valley and echoed against the riverbank. He pushed the shifter into fifth gear and let out the clutch as he pushed on the gas pedal. He grinned at the speedometer and then decided to stop his acceleration and let gravity and resistance, slow him down.

It was nearly dark now, as the car began slowing down. The scenery flew past as the car continued to speed along the road while decelerating. No police lights had come up from behind him. All he had to do now was slow down to the speed limit and take the curve up ahead. Dave's pulse began to slow down too, as he realized he had gotten away with speeding. After all, he thought, what was the good of having a turbocharged, intercooled 1.3-liter rotary engine if you couldn't use it?

That was when his eyes caught a dark shape moving at him from the right. In a fraction of a second, Dave saw the two eyes shining back at him as the deer ran in front of his car. There was no time to stop, though Dave hit the

Cottonwood
By Kevin J. Curtis

brakes just before the deer came crashing into the right front of the car. The animal hit the bumper and its body broke open upon impact. The head and part of the body hit the right side of the windshield and broke the glass in a spider-web pattern before it shattered, falling into the car with the animal's head. Blood and glass were intermixed, and blood was smeared across the pavement. Two delicate legs with hooves still intact were separated from the rest of the body of the animal and lay in the road. Part of the back half of the body was crushed and lying in the road. The ribcage was partially exposed and some of the intestines hung out.

    Dave lost control of the car, and it left the road and went into the ditch. Dave had been wearing a seatbelt, and the airbag had deployed and saved him from major head trauma. There were some skid marks on the pavement, though the antilock brakes had successfully reduced much of the skidding that may have otherwise occurred.

    There was no evidence after-the-fact that Dave had been speeding. By the time of the accident, he had slowed to almost the posted speed limit. At fifty-five miles per hour,[20] it had still been enough to mutilate the deer, damage the car, injure Dave and send the car off the highway into the ditch.

    The aftermath was strangely calm and almost serene, as the silence drifted in around the accident scene. The sky was dark now. The Mazda's lights were still on, though the right front end of the car was damaged and the headlight on that side was broken.

    Dave felt as if he was outside of his body for a few moments. His vision was dark, and his hearing sounded compressed, as if he was inside of a tunnel. Slowly, as the pain in his head became more intense as the initial shock began to wear off, his vision began to return as he blinked

Cottonwood
By Kevin J. Curtis

the blood out of his eyes. In spite of a dull ringing in his ears, Dave's hearing began to return as well.

His body hurt and his face stung. He began to assess his situation. He could see out of both eyes now, which seemed amazing when he noticed the damage to his windshield. Glass lay blasted across the whole interior of the car. Something was pushing on his chest. Dave managed to move his right arm to the spot, and he grabbed hold of something. It was hard… and smooth… an antler!

He pulled the antler away from his body with some pain and difficulty, before realizing it was the head of the deer! He leaned over and vomited, which served to make the mess inside the Mazda even more disgusting. He tried to open the driver's side door, but it was stuck shut. Across the right side of the car, the remains of the deer blocked the way out. He was too weak and injured to struggle anymore.

He lay there for sometime, wondering if he could get out. As the mosquitoes entered the bloody car and began to feed on his face and body, he wondered if it was such a good idea to get out. Certainly, the insects would be worse outside of the vehicle. But what about the danger of fire? He could smell gasoline now. What if the car caught on fire and he was trapped inside?

Panic set in momentarily, until he calmed himself by the realization that he had been trapped here for sometime and nothing had started burning. He reached up to rub the mosquitoes from his bloodstained face. Once, he even thought he heard a car go by.

Eventually, he did hear someone outside. He noticed the pulsing lights flashing from somewhere in the darkness. Then a flashlight shined through the window.

"Keep calm there, buddy, help is on the way," a man's voice said. It continued a little farther away now, "I need an ambulance, fire truck and a tow truck out on Black Dog Road, just west of the power plant. I have one male

Cottonwood
By Kevin J. Curtis

victim in a car/deer crash who needs medical attention, over." There was the sound of a radio transmission, as Dave felt himself losing consciousness.

"Stay with me buddy," the voice said, a bit louder now as the police officer tried to assess the situation. He knew that Dave was hurt, but he also knew that it was better not to move him.

"The firemen are on the way to cut you out of this rig. We'll have you to a hospital in no time," the officer said, trying to reassure the bloody man in the broken car.

Off in the distance, sirens could be heard. The sound was coming from two directions and getting louder. Dave could hear that each siren had its own sound, and neither were the same. He listened to them getting closer, until the noise was almost deafening. Then it all stopped. He could hear doors opening and men shouting to each other. Then a new voice said,

"We'll have you out of there in a couple of minutes, hang tight."

Dave could hear a machine start up. Then he could hear the sound of metal crunching. All at once, the side of the car was open. People were holding him down and strapping something around his neck. Then they counted to three and lifted him from the wreckage. They strapped him to a board and loaded him into an ambulance.

The door closed and the siren outside started back up again.
"We'll be there in a few minutes," a voice said.

Cottonwood
By Kevin J. Curtis

Chapter 22: Inhabitants

The cottonwood tree continued to grow larger. By now, it had roots that extended beyond the riverbank and into the river itself. The tree had now grown to a width of two and one half feet.[3]

As spring returned to the river valley, the snow began to melt. With it, water rushed from the roadways and ended up in the watershed ponds and eventually into the lakes and rivers. Untold numbers of chemicals were washed into these waterways, along with a disgusting amount of manmade trash.

The two hikers, a man and woman, dressed in waterproof boots, walked along the series of watersheds known as the Bass Ponds. This area had been used in the early half of the twentieth century, as a place to grow game fish to a size where they could be used to stock other lakes and waterways. A spring fed into the ponds and the cold, clean water had supported among other things, Brown Trout. With the building of the highway, bridges, roadways and buildings nearby, the Bass Ponds became both polluted, and a nature study area and eventually it was included into the Minnesota Valley National Wildlife Refuge.

The two hikers decided to walk around the first pond, closest to the Cedar Freeway. They were amazed, and saddened by the quantity of garbage littering the area. Both in the water, and well out onto the land, there were untold numbers of plastic articles, bottles, cans, and even pill bottles and syringes.

There were also the "party spots," with beer bottles and cans, but the quantity and distribution of garbage led one to believe that much of it had been transported with the water runoff from the roads and freeway. If this much garbage was on the land, likely placed there by receding

Cottonwood
By Kevin J. Curtis

floodwaters, how much more trash was under the water in these ponds?

Wildlife still existed here, as evidenced by the muskrats, Mallards, Goldeneyes, Mergansers and Canada Geese in the ponds. However, they were obviously not immune to the "toxic soup" that they were swimming in. That was evident by the quantity of dead fish rotting on the shoreline.

The hikers watched as large, Golden Shiners swam near the surface. Their bodies looked distorted by sores and skin eruptions. Some floated dead, upside-down. The edge of the pond was littered by hundreds of their decomposing bodies.

Even if the (human) neighbors organized and picked up the litter, they would never be able to clean it all up. The deadly chemicals were taking their toll. Perhaps the toxins would begin to affect the migratory waterfowl that were swimming in the foul waters of the pond. Who could know how far the effects would extend?

* * * *

When the weather warmed up, the neighborhood children were released from school for the summer. John and his friend Mike had just finished sixth grade, and the summer was a welcome change from sitting in a schoolroom. They had their bikes, and rode on the old dirt trail leading through the woods and along the river.

The bottomland forest was the perfect place for adventures, and the two friends were always on the lookout for some fun or mischief to get into. They stopped, and dropped their bikes to the ground near the river's edge. They had brought fishing poles, but first they proceeded to throw rocks into the rushing current of the river.

Had their fathers been present, the boys would have been scolded for "scaring the fish away" with their rock

Cottonwood
By Kevin J. Curtis

throwing. There were no parents here, however, and they could do as they wished. When they grew tired of skipping stones and throwing rocks, they set about the task of locating some worms for bait. After rolling a few dead logs over, they managed to find a few worms to use for their afternoon fishing expedition.

    The weather was already hot, and the fish weren't biting. Soon the two boys became bored, and they started pushing each other. After falling into the mud on the riverbank, they nearly rolled into the river, which may have been disastrous. They were able to avoid the water and swift current, however, and they soon packed up their fishing gear and were speeding away on their bicycles.

    As evening approached, a group of teenagers appeared along the river. They were nearby where the cottonwood tree was growing. They were some distance off the trail, and so they felt safe enough to have a party. One of the teens had had his older brother buy beer for him. All of those present were underage, and even if they weren't, alcohol consumption was prohibited in the wildlife refuge. They started a fire in a fire pit that they constructed. It was a nice small fire, but as they drank more beer and started smoking marijuana, the fire kept getting bigger. One of the boys was adding more and more wood.

    By morning, the fire was burned out and the partiers were gone. The beer cans were strewn about the area. A glass bottle was shattered against a tree, and shards of glass lay on the ground beneath it. This was not an isolated incident. The warm weather brought the partiers into the river valley. Unfortunately, they usually left their trash behind.

    Later that summer, a group of volunteers hiked through. One of them noticed the trash left behind by the partiers. Much of the garbage was cleaned up, though

Cottonwood
By Kevin J. Curtis

broken glass remained behind. In the river, more garbage was under the water, where it had been thrown.

* * * *

The season was dry, and the river was low. The large cottonwoods still flourished, as they were usually growing in close proximity to water. The various lakes and marshes were drying up in the dry summer heat. Long Meadow Lake was no exception. Fish were forced to congregate in the areas that held enough water for them to live comfortably. One of these places was a pond that was created by a family of beavers.

The surrounding marsh was green with duckweed and algae, yet the waters of the beaver pond were relatively clear. There was a drainage runoff, as this area served as a watershed for the surrounding human settlements. This running water was attractive to the beavers, even though they did not have to build a dam here. What they did construct, was a large lodge as their living quarters. They also had to create canals, used to move logs and branches. In the process, they excavated the area to support their activities and allow them to bury a stockpile of branches (with tender bark) for food, and access to the lodge from underneath–below the surface of the water.

This small ecosystem within the larger ecosystem was a perfect habitat for a variety of fish. Because of this, other animals visited the area to find food, such as raccoons, otters and herons. While carp and bullheads were numerous in the lake, the beaver pond was dominated by sunfish, bass and a few Pickerel.

The area was somewhat protected from human intrusion, due to the saturated ground in the vicinity, and the potential to sink in the mud if you put too much weight in too small of an area. After exploring the area, however, a man decided that he had to return with his fishing gear on

Cottonwood
By Kevin J. Curtis

another day. His exploration of the beaver lodge and surrounding area showed a large population of fish, some quite large–that were visible in the relatively clear water when the sun was shining. Two days later, he returned with fishing gear and his girlfriend, and over the next three hours, they managed to fill their stringer with bass and sunfish.

It seemed funny that such a small, pool of water, would have so much potential for fishing. Usually shore fishing was not too successful. This, it seemed, was a true "fishing hole." There was a bit of mud to navigate, but the full stringer only told half the story. Many fish were released during the process. Worms and crappie minnows were the bait used.

As they hiked back out to their car, the man told his girlfriend to keep this fishing spot a secret. It was too hard to find a good place that was not full of people. Too often, these people took too many fish, and left garbage in and around the lake. She agreed, and they went home to enjoy a meal of fresh fish.

* * * *

It was late in May of 2002. A female cougar had wandered out of the bottomland forest, into a city park in Bloomington, Minnesota. She had been wandering along the river valley, as these cats sometimes did. There was plenty of food for them down in the valley. There were deer, raccoons, and plenty of other animals that could be used for food by a mountain lion.

This cat wasn't particularly large at ninety pounds[21] but it was large enough to scare some pedestrians who saw it as they were walking on a path through the park. The walkers called police, and soon officers arrived on the scene.

Cottonwood
By Kevin J. Curtis

For several minutes, the police officers tried to scare the big cat away. The cougar was hiding in some brush, and it wouldn't leave in spite of the officers who threw branches at it and shined flashlights in the area. It was just after dark, and the cougar apparently saw no real reason that it should leave. Eventually, the police officers shot the animal repeatedly until they killed it.

The cougar had been traveling for many days. She had wandered along the river, looking for new territory. She was a young animal, and weighed about ninety pounds. She had found plenty of food in the river valley. Most recently, she had stalked a small group of turkeys, and had managed to kill an old tom. That was yesterday, and she had traveled several miles since then.

She had encountered another cougar's territory less than two miles[22] west of here. When she encountered the marked area, she fled. The resident cat was large, and had established a territory in the woods near the grain elevators of a private corporation.

This cat had been searching for her own territory and had eventually wandered into a city park. This park had considerable natural areas, and a walking path that led some human beings into the area where the cougar was hiding.

The large cat was somewhat disoriented and scared. Earlier, she had fled from the sound of dogs barking when she approached a residential area. She wasn't sure where to run, and for the moment, the brush she was crouched in seemed to be her safest choice.

Soon more humans arrived, and she continued to growl her warning as they threw things at her and shined lights at her. Suddenly she felt a sharp pain, as something penetrated her body. She felt it again, and jumped from her hiding place–lunging in the direction of her assailants.

Cottonwood
By Kevin J. Curtis

There was more pain and she kept hearing the loud crack of gunshot reports.

She fell to the ground a short distance from her persecutors. She could feel the pain in her body. She could smell her own blood. She screamed one last time at her enemies before she collapsed and died.

The police examined the cougar that they had just killed. One wondered why it didn't leave when they tried to scare it away. Another mentioned that they *"had to kill it."* This lone cat had been found guilty of being a potential danger to the thousands of people nearby. There was no trial, just an execution.

The next day, as Maureen walked her dog through the same park, she thought about the story that she saw on the television news that morning. Her dog was small. It was a shaggy, mixed breed that would be but a morsel for a mountain lion she thought. Maureen eyed the brush and felt an involuntary shudder as she hurried her little dog along. There was *no way* she was going to be out here after dark anymore!

People like Maureen had gotten comfortable with the thought that dangerous animals such as cougars no longer lived this close to the city. What about this one? Could anyone really know that there weren't any more living in the woods around the park?

Other people were also upset by the story. Some felt that it would be a remarkable thing to see a wild cougar. They were angry that the animal was killed. It seemed to them that this was the response that happened all too often. They wondered why the cat couldn't be tranquilized and moved.

Some naturalists believed that moving a cougar into the territory occupied by another, might be sentencing it to death anyway. There was also the time and expense of

Cottonwood
By Kevin J. Curtis

dealing with the animal. Some people believed that any potentially dangerous animal should be killed. Eventually, time passed and so did the debate about what should have been done.

* * * *

He wasn't one of the "hardcore" bicyclists who dressed in spandex and wore a helmet. He wasn't into it on that scale. He did have a pretty good bicycle. He'd been able to trade his sick time for it at a previous job, and decided that it was a good investment. He'd gotten a helmet at the same time, but he never wore it. He knew it was safer, but he had shaved his head some years back, and would need a "do-rag" to block the sun from shining through the vents, and to and make it comfortable. He preferred a snug fitting baseball style cap.

His favorite trek was not for the novice. Though he only got out a few times each year, it was a grueling journey that typically took three or four hours. It started at the top of the river valley in Burnsville, and went down a steep hill along Nicollet Avenue heading north. At the bottom, he followed a paved path that went parallel to Interstate 35W. On the other side, he was on the west end of Black Dog Road, which he followed past the power plant and into Fort Snelling State Park. From there he might continue to Mendota, where he would stop at the historic Sibley House for a rest in the yard, or he could buy a pop from the Mendota Mdewakanton Dakota Community store.

Other times he would climb the hill at Interstate 494 by Gun Club Lake, and then ride up the grade to the headquarters of the Minnesota Valley National Wildlife Refuge. After stopping for a rest there, he would return through the Long Meadow Lake Unit of the refuge. Usually at least once during these rides, he had to cross the

Cottonwood
By Kevin J. Curtis

Minnesota River under the pedestrian pass that was below the "new" Cedar (Hwy 77) bridge. The old bridge was still visible to the east of the new bridge, but it was closed due to structural failure.

Today's bike trip led him to a close view of a Bald Eagle on the west side of Black Dog Lake. Later, in the state park, he scared up a few deer as he peddled along the trail. The wildlife refuge headquarters was a great spot to view wild turkeys, as they had grown somewhat tame and spent considerable time at the birdfeeders.

The trip was usually in excess of twenty miles, ending with a grueling ride uphill, out of the river valley. By the time he was back home, he was exhausted, hot and very thirsty. The one bottle of water attached to his bike was insufficient for such a ride–especially in summer heat.

Along the way, he would see other riders. Some of them were casual about the experience, and most chose to transport their bicycles by motor vehicle to their starting location. Some were outfitted with the latest apparel and had bikes with shock absorbers and the latest technology. All seemed to enjoy the experience of biking in the river valley.

Chapter 23: Deadly Finds

The usual serenity of this woodsy, city park was suddenly shattered. Someone had found the partially clothed body of a woman hidden beneath the trees, and now, Bloomington Police, the Hennepin County Coroner's Office, and a variety of spectators filled the area. The police held the crowd back beyond the yellow tape that defined the crime scene.

Moir Park was large, and expanded from the usual park amenities into a number of hiking trails that connected to those of both the *Bloomington Greenspace,* and the

Cottonwood
By Kevin J. Curtis

Minnesota Valley National Wildlife Refuge. While this was a fantastic area for recreation, it also afforded those with malevolent intentions, adequate room and cover for anonymity. Rarely did such a thing occur as this, however.

Speculation was that the victim was a young woman who was missing. The coroner's office would eventually confirm this, along with an autopsy report that confirmed that she had been murdered. The newspapers and television news covered the story at length, though not much beyond this was ever found out.

She had disappeared sometime earlier, and efforts were made to determine what had happened to her. Later, there would be suspects brought in and questioned. Still, in the end, the murder of this young woman would continue to remain unsolved. There would even be speculation that yet another man, with ties to the area may have killed her. This, after the man was convicted of the murder of another young woman, when her bone fragments were found in a fire-pit on land belonging to him.

Over time, the huge psychological impact that these high-profile crimes would have on the community would slowly evaporate into the valley; the way a summer rain does when the fog can be seen rising off the sun heated ground.

After thousands of years of human activity in the river valley, the worst of humanity was always as ready as the best of humanity to show its face. Even during the last two or three centuries, much good and evil had laid its will upon this valley and all that lived nearby. The cottonwoods continued to grow, despite the horrors they had witnessed. Silently, they held the secrets that some of the humans tried to hide within their forest.

* * * * *

Cottonwood
By Kevin J. Curtis

They drove off the road in the dark, onto a seldom-used dirt incline that the hunters used in the fall to park before hiking in to hunt deer and waterfowl. Only these men weren't hunting. They were up to a much more sinister activity.

One of them had already scouted out the area, and he led the way. They wouldn't be going into the woods very far. They carried black, plastic garbage bags that were tied shut. Inside of each bag, there were such things as empty or near empty containers from brake fluid, drain cleaner, paint thinner, acetone, alcohol, and antifreeze. There were compressed gas cylinders, alkaline batteries, empty packages of cold medicine like, pseudoephedrine and ephedrine. The bags contained old coffee filters, rock salt, anhydrous ammonia, and red stained bed sheets. This was extremely toxic material.

These two men were cooks. What they were cooking, however, was methamphetamines. The materials used to make this drug were extremely toxic. The garbage produced, also toxic, was a telltale sign to anyone in law enforcement, and a growing number of well informed citizens. Therefore, these two men were making an illegal dump of garbage into the wildlife refuge.

Once they had unloaded the bags of toxic waste, they got back into their truck and drove up the incline and back onto the road. The whole process had taken only a few minutes. Once they were driving, the passenger pulled out a glass pipe and filled it with a small white rock. He lit it and inhaled. Then he passed the apparatus over to the driver, while he held the lighter to the bowl.

The next morning, as the heat of the sun hit the black plastic bags, they began to inflate with toxic fumes. Two days later, the plastic was compromised, and toxic liquid was leaking into the ground. Two weeks later, the

Cottonwood
By Kevin J. Curtis

chemicals were running into the nearby creek, with the runoff of the rain.

After three weeks, a volunteer from the wildlife refuge was hiking along a little used area of the refuge lands. He spotted the black plastic bags, and knew that whatever this was, it wasn't good. He approached to see if he could determine what was inside without opening them. He always had a fear that someday he would find a dead body or something truly horrible.

When he got closer, he saw that some of the bags were ripped open and he smelled the sweet, chemical odor, and recognized the items that were visible–from a training session that he had attended at the refuge headquarters. This was a meth dump. He pulled out his cell phone, and dialed the wildlife refuge headquarters, to report the find.

The call was transferred to the law enforcement officer, who cautioned the volunteer to stay away from the garbage. The location of the dump site was described in detail to the officer, who keyed the information into his laptop computer. Later that day, the officer visited the site himself. He contacted the local law enforcement authorities, and by the next day, there was a HAZMAT team at the site.

The crew wore white suits with hoods and breathing apparatus. They loaded the bags and refuse carefully into containers and then they proceeded to take the accompanying top layer of soil. Tests were done on the soil and the creek water to determine the extent of contamination.

In the end, there *was* contamination to the site. Since it was away from human habitation, little more was done to correct it. It was fortunate that the volunteer had found the dump when he did, to minimize the damage from contamination. Later that summer, there were frogs and fish lying dead on the side of the creek. They had succumbed to

Cottonwood
By Kevin J. Curtis

the devastating effects of the poisons left behind by the meth cooks.

* * * *

Lyle had lost his job. That was two weeks ago. He was having little luck finding new employment. He did what he thought he needed to do. He looked through the newspaper's job ads. He went to the Workforce Center. He even went on an interview, and later nothing happened. When he finally called the potential employer, he found that he was "no longer being considered." Each day, he grew more depressed as his prospects seemed to dim, and his bills continued to grow.

His family offered what help and encouragement that they could. He was thirty-six, unmarried and was facing the prospect of moving back into his parent's basement. This combination of events was proving to be more than Lyle could deal with. He looked around his little apartment, at the boxes and the job of moving that lay before him. He had no ambition for this. He eyed the half-full bottle of cheap vodka sitting on the table.

The television droned on in the background. There was some crap on. It was just another one of those stupid reality shows. He took a hard drink off of the bottle. Then he took a few more. Soon the bottle was empty.

Lyle decided that he would go buy some more. He needed cigarettes too. He stood up, stumbled a bit and then put on his shirt and shoes and locked his apartment door behind him. He stopped outside, and then unlocked his door and went back in. He came back out wearing a jacket. Inside the pocket, he had his handgun. It was a .38, snub-nose revolver. He wasn't sure exactly what he was going to do, but he felt a certain finality about it.

He stepped outside into the warm evening air. The sky was still light, though the last remnants of daylight

Cottonwood
By Kevin J. Curtis

were vanishing quickly. The summer days were long, and as he walked along the edge of the highway, he thought about running into traffic and ending his miserable existence.

He reached the liquor store, where he bought another bottle of cheap vodka, a pack of smokes and a sixteen-ounce bottle of Coke. He crossed the highway, not toward home, but toward the river. He entered the thick growth and emerged out the other side. Ahead of him were the railroad tracks, elevated on a manmade ridge, and running either direction, as far as he could see. He climbed up and began walking along the railroad tracks.

He lit a cigarette and opened his bottle of vodka. Off in the distance, he could hear the sound of a train. He wondered what would happen if he laid down on the tracks and went to sleep. After walking about a half mile, he left the tracks and headed into a woodsy area next to the swampland.

Once inside the woods, he found a cottonwood tree that seemed like a good place to sit down and lean against. The mosquitoes were attracted to him, as he was sweating and exhaling carbon dioxide. He thought about the "ancient" spray can of insect repellent on the shelf of his closet at home. It only figured that the one time he might actually have need of it, he wouldn't have it with him.

He sat there; smoking cigarettes and drinking vodka like it was the last thing he would ever get to do. He chased down the strong liquor with intermittent sips of Coke. Eventually, he took little notice of the mosquitoes that were feasting on his evermore intoxicating blood.

There in that place, all alone, Lyle came to a decision that would affect his life forever after. He decided that he couldn't move back to his parent's basement. He decided that he would never find another job. He felt like no one cared that much if he was here or gone.

Cottonwood
By Kevin J. Curtis

That was it! He would leave. There was no reason that he had to stay here in this city. He was now free to go anywhere! His head felt funny and the liquor was burning his stomach. The two pieces of old pizza he'd eaten four hours earlier wasn't holding him over. He looked up at the huge tree overhead. It started spinning. His stomach began rolling. He leaned over to the side and vomited out the poison that was in his stomach.

After he finished, he leaned back against the tree and decided that he would have a hell of a hangover tomorrow. Then, he lit another cigarette and took a deep inhale of it. He blew out and watched the smoke rise slowly into the damp air. Then he reached into his pocket and pulled out the .38. He held it against the side of his head and pulled the trigger.

* * * *

The evening news on this particular night featured a story that was also carried by the newspapers. A man had disappeared one night. His family was upset and wanted answers. The police were taking it seriously, yet there was no evidence of foul play, and the individual may have just left town.

There was no note, no message–he was just gone. His sister was shown on television, pleading with anyone who might know where "Lyle" had gone. She said that he had been depressed about losing his job, and he may have walked off into the river bottoms. There was a brief search of the surrounding areas, but nothing was discovered.

* * * *

Bill was walking his dog in the cool of the morning. It was commonplace, as the Labrador had abundant energy, and was better behaved when exercised frequently. They were walking along the railroad tracks, and Bill was careful

Cottonwood
By Kevin J. Curtis

to listen and watch incase a train came by. Usually, there was no train, but this morning it came early, and Bill and his dog left the ridge where the rail-line was, and moved off into a small area of trees next to the marsh, to wait until the train had passed.

Once in the woods, Bill decided to risk the $250 fine for having an unleashed dog in the wildlife refuge. It was extremely unlikely that anyone would be out here at 6:00AM on a Saturday. He let the dog loose as the train roared past and was gone. Once freed, the dog had all kinds of "dog stuff" to do, which included smelling and investigating everything.

Eventually Bill had to call the dog, because he had run too far away, and was busily "working" an area as if he had found something. The man was forced to walk over to the dog to retrieve him. Once he got close, Bill saw what the dog had found. He called sharply and the dog finally stopped smelling the corpse and trotted back to his owner. Bill quickly reattached the leash to the Labrador's collar, and reached for his cell phone. The phone was missing.

Apparently, he had been in such a hurry to enjoy the morning with his dog, that he had forgotten the phone. Now, all he could do was quickly head back home and call the police from there. As he hurried away, Bill looked back over his shoulder to try to remember the location. As he walked home, he could not shake the awful memory of the badly decomposed body, and the smell of death that filled the surrounding air. If not visually, one would be able to find the body by the smell.

His wife was still in bed when he got home. He told her what he had found, and she was horrified. She quickly got dressed, while her husband called the local police. An hour later, Bill was once again, standing on the railroad tracks, as uniformed officers walked into the area he had pointed out. After verifying the gruesome discovery, they

Cottonwood
By Kevin J. Curtis

contacted the county coroner's office to come and retrieve the body.

The police finished asking Bill questions to put into their reports. He told of how his dog had made the discovery after they left the tracks to let the train pass by. After the officers finished, they said that Bill could go home. As he walked back to his house, he wondered how he could ever go walking in that area again. He had never seen anything as ghastly as that decomposing, and animal scavenged body. He knew that this event would leave him changed forever.

Later that week, Bill returned to his normal, daily life. He would never forget what had happened on that Saturday morning. He had managed to walk the same route once since then, but he did not let his dog off the leash this time, and he had no desire to leave the railroad tracks again. Fortunately, no trains had come during this walk.

He had received a follow-up call from the police. The body had been that of a man named Lyle. Apparently, he had died from a self-inflicted gunshot wound to his head. Later that evening, on the television news, the follow-up story, along with a picture of Lyle, told of what had happened to the man who had disappeared three weeks earlier. Bill stared at the face on the television screen. The face of Lyle in the picture was not the face that he had seen in the woods. He decided to try to remember the way Lyle had looked in life, while knowing that he would never forget how he had looked in death.

Cottonwood
By Kevin J. Curtis

Chapter 24: Survival Hunt
  Hundreds of years in the past, a small group of hunters were searching for woodland bison or caribou. These prehistoric men occupied the land within the valley that would much later be called, the Minnesota River Valley. The climate of the time was somewhat dryer and warmer, though the cold of winter presented great challenges for the survival of these men and their families. There were no weaklings among these people. Individuals with deformities, or who were severely injured or took ill were systematically weeded out by the pressures of survival.

  Armed with spears and atlatls,[18] these hunters were extremely talented in the art of survival. There was **no** means of obtaining food, shelter and clothing, except by their own skills, courage and perseverance. Perhaps one should also mention that a good dose of luck was also needed. In the end though, it was their knowledge of the environment, and their craftsmanship in creating weapons, that had a direct correlation as to whether they lived or died. Back in their village, the women and children also depended on the hunting skills of these men, just as the men depended on the skills and labor of the women to ensure their survival in the primeval wilderness.

  Spears were a common way to hunt for large game. One of the difficulties of this weapon, was that a man needed to get rather close to an animal to be able to accurately throw a spear into it. One of the early technological advancements to compensate for this, was the invention of the atlatl.

  An atlatl was a device that essentially "elongated" the throwing arm of an individual, making it as if he were far taller and larger than a typical man. The darts or small spears that were propelled by this device flew much farther

Cottonwood
By Kevin J. Curtis

and with significantly more power than a spear would. Such a device also required a certain amount of skill to utilize with any accuracy, yet these men had mastered this weapon and used it to improve their success rate in the hunting of large game.

The skills of these hunters should not be understated. Since their main occupation revolved around the use of weapons to provide meat and protection for their families, these skills were practiced to a point that is difficult to understand in the modern world. Modern weapons are easier to use and master, though most individuals who might use them, are employed in other occupations that require much of their time.

In no way are modern humans superior to these early people, as they survived in the wilderness by knowledge, skill, cunning and adaptation. Those who did not possess such attributes were culled via *natural selection.* There were limited resources to care for the injured or sick, though there is some evidence that this was done.

One common problem that is easily corrected for modern human beings, is the condition of poor visual acuity. There are glasses, contact lenses, or laser surgery to correct most of these deficiencies. Prehistoric humans had no such ways to compensate. A man with visual difficulties would be disadvantaged as a hunter. His collaboration with others, who perhaps had stronger vision, would increase his likelihood of surviving.

The health issues of the five men actively pursuing game with their atlatls could not be known at the time, except to say that none of them would survive much beyond three decades of life. This shortened lifespan was mostly for reasons of injury and disease–much of which is no longer deadly in the modern world due to advances in medicine.

Cottonwood
By Kevin J. Curtis

The leader of this band of hunters was a powerful man who had survived to the age of twenty-two. At this age, he was in good health and still void of the problems of his father, who had died of the complications of aging that had caught up with him the previous winter. The leader had two wives and five children. He had fathered eleven children in all, but six had already passed on by this point in time.

The five men of this hunting party were all related either by blood or marriage. They all lived with their wives and children, in a collective group that worked together for the benefit of all. They were nomadic by nature, following the migration patterns of the animals they hunted.

The women of this extended family were expert in finding edible roots, berries and other plants. They also captured small animals such as rodents, crayfish and certain insects that provided an important part of their diet. The women were also responsible for most of the domestic chores, such as making clothing, curing hides and preserving food. They were indispensable to the functioning of the group.

The children were indoctrinated early into the roles assigned to their gender. Childhood was short and so was the typical lifespan by modern standards. These people did not have the luxury of waiting for the "right moment." Those moments were fleeting in nature, and time stood still for no one. In short, these people were as wild as the land they lived in and the animals that they hunted, and for this reason, they were able to survive.

Hundreds of years later, we cannot fully grasp what life was like back then. Even when we go camping in the wildest areas yet remaining, we almost always have modern equipment to back us up. It is also safe to surmise that the large predators were more numerous and less afraid of humans in prehistoric times. Even in the written account

Cottonwood
By Kevin J. Curtis

of Marco Polo's (1254-1324) adventures, he mentioned that lions might sometimes attack humans. The natural tendency of animals to flee from humanity is likely a behavior that was acquired over time and increased contact with armed Homo sapiens.

In this particular culture, the atlatl was "cutting-edge" technology. Fire was something to be feared when it was out-of-control, yet the benefits of controlled fire were obvious in heat, cooked food, and keeping back predatory animals in the darkness. Despite many primitive advances, herbal and shamanistic healing was often unable to keep people from dying from common maladies that modern medicine would later easily manage.

Infection was, no doubt, one of the biggest killers of the time. The transfer of disease from individual to individual in a world without antibiotics, could mean that anyone, and particularly the young and the old, were susceptible to deadly bacterial infections.

Injuries could also become infected. Broken bones would heal in strange directions, and severe puncture wounds would likely cause the victim to bleed to death. It was also likely that cancer, heart attacks and strokes were uncommon at the time, as these maladies are more common in the elderly, and few people were likely to reach old age in prehistoric times.

As the five hunters stalked a group of woodland bison, they used the tactic of splitting up and surrounding their prey. This is a specialized, collaborative way to hunt, and stealth, cooperation and patience are skills that must be incorporated. Generally, one group or individual would position himself to be discovered and cause the animals to flee in the direction of a waiting ambush. When possible, they might use a natural feature of the landscape to increase their success, such as a muddy bog to entangle their hoofed prey, or perhaps a cliff that they could run the panicked

Cottonwood
By Kevin J. Curtis

animals over the edge of. This tactic was safer for the hunters, as it allowed for the animals to be killed by the fall, rather than in a close-quarter battle.

The small herd of bison was not near such a natural entrapment, and the hunters would have to rely on their skills with the atlatls to bring down their prey. The youngest man, a boy by modern standards, moved quietly through the woodland growth to flank the animals and ultimately cause them to panic and run toward the other hunters.

On the last occasion that these hunters attempted this maneuver, they were surprised by a group of wolves that took the chase away from them and drove the herd away. The wolves were successful in bringing down a young cow, but they were in no mood to share and successfully drove the humans away as well.

As the boy worked his way into position, the other men spread out and waited in ambush. The leader sat motionless in the brush, as mosquitoes buzzed around him. The insects were part of life for these men, and he took little notice of them–even when they were actively feeding on his blood. He did divert his focus momentarily, as he found an engorged tick hanging from the back of his thigh. He pulled the insect loose, leaving its head still stuck in his skin. This would eventually cause a skin irritation as his body pushed the foreign substance to the surface and out.

In a few more minutes, the boy had stampeded the bison toward his fellow hunters. As the animals ran past, the hunters had to utilize the brush and trees to step out of the way and avoid being crushed. This they accomplished, while also firing their darts, propelled by the atlatls. Having hit two of the animals, one simply kept running, while the other fell and instantly leapt back to its feet. By this time, the hunters had launched a barrage of spears into the beast,

Cottonwood
By Kevin J. Curtis

which now took on a new role as it aggressively ran at the attackers.

The hunters stayed cautious, as these animals were sometimes known to return and attack, especially if a young animal was being pursued. It was sometime between the last volley of darts and spears, and the final blow delivered by the leader with an axe made of the thigh bone of a large animal, that the group noticed the young bull running away, toward the rest of the herd. The other animals were already long gone, and the bull had come from the direction of the boy who had initiated the stampede.

When they reached him, the boy could not speak. He had been gored and trampled by the enraged bull. He lay broken on the ground. The leader had tears in his eyes as he ordered the other three men to butcher the fallen bison, while he stooped to lift his fallen son onto his shoulders to carry him back to the village.

Later, when all were back, the smell of meat roasting filled the air. Women worked on the hide of the bison and prepared strips of meat for drying. The people had found ways to use nearly the entirety of the animal. Nearby, the boy lay comatose. His wounds were severe, and the damage was complicated by the trip back to the village. He died in the night.

The next morning, after much wailing by his mother, the family, including his father, who was painted in the colors of death, tied the boy's body to a gnarled old cottonwood tree on a hill above the river. There his body would stay, until such time as his remaining bones would be collected and buried in the "place of the dead."

The life of these people was difficult and often harsh. There were no storybook endings here. Their lives mirrored the lives of the animals that inhabited the same land that they lived in. If one was fortunate, he or she could

Cottonwood
By Kevin J. Curtis

survive youth and perhaps even dominate for a time. This period of being in the prime of life, was usually fleeting before another, younger, stronger individual took over either by force, or by the elder relinquishing his position. This could be followed by either a violent death, or a slower one, caused by maladies related to aging.

They lived and died, and no books were written to record their lives or achievements. Sometimes one might survive for a time, in an oral history. These stories were by nature, subject to changes as they were passed down from person to person and from generation to generation. Often, individual distinctions were blurred into others, until a heroic figure emerged out of the deeds of several generations.

Other times, the entire clan could be wiped out in a clash with an enemy clan. Survivors were generally either executed, or they became slaves or members of the victors' families. If the family did survive the centuries, time and generations brought changes that would prove to be both good and bad. Eventually, it would be extremely difficult for modern human beings to understand or survive such a lifestyle.

Chapter 25: The Hunt

Dale had been a hunter since shortly after his twelfth birthday. That was when his dad enrolled him in a firearms safety course, and then the two went hunting for deer that fall. It wasn't until he was fourteen, when Dale actually shot his first deer. It was a six-point buck, and he couldn't have been prouder.

That was a long time ago, and Dale's dad, Earl, didn't hunt anymore. He was getting too "long in the tooth," as he would say–to spend hours out in the cold and damp waiting for a deer to come along.

Cottonwood
By Kevin J. Curtis

Things had changed since that first hunt. Dale had given up hunting with his rifle, in favor of using a bow and arrows. Another difference was that shooting does (as opposed to bucks) was now encouraged, because the deer population was getting too high in many places; particularly those areas that were in close proximity to human settlements.

The equipment had changed over the years as well. While firearms hunters wore blaze-orange, bow hunters were more apt to use camouflage. Dale was outfitted in space-age materials that were lightweight, warm, and let perspiration escape while retaining warmth. His boots were waterproof, and he wore gators to protect his legs from the icy waters of the marshes where he hunted.

The bow and arrows were nothing like those used by the American Indians, who hunted these same woods and marshlands in the past. Dale's *compound bow* bore little resemblance to the longbows, short bows and recurve bows of the past. Recurves were still made, though usually of fiberglass, but they were not nearly as powerful or accurate as the compound bows.

The compound bows used a system of pulleys to increase the power and decrease the recoil of the bow. Once it was "broke," the bow was easy to hold in the ready-to-fire position. There was also a trigger that held the bowstring and reduced the movement caused by manually releasing it. In short, it was something of a hybrid of what a bow used to be, and what it turned into by using new technology to improve an ancient weapon.

The arrows, were made of hollow, aluminum shafts, nylon flight guides (instead of feathers), and wicked steel tips that were razor sharp and barbed. Such an arrow would obviously create a deadly wound, especially when fired with the power and accuracy afforded by a compound bow in the hands of a skilled hunter.

Cottonwood
By Kevin J. Curtis

Recently, Dale's brother-in-law, Sang, became interested in bow hunting as well. Sang had been an avid hunter and fisherman since his family's arrival to the United States, back in 1979. He had mostly hunted small game, but he was very interested in deer hunting when Dale was talking about it. Sang had recently invested in a compound bow and he was excited about hunting with his brother-in-law.

Dale was happy to have someone to go hunting with him. Time could drag into long hours when waiting to ambush deer. There was also the added advantage of having a second person along if there was an accident, or to help drag the deer out of the woods or marsh after it was killed. Deer had a way of running into the densest brush or muddiest areas to die.

Dale had told Sang of his previous year's experience. He had gone evenings and weekends over the long bow season, and had not gotten a deer until the end. The weather had been warmer than average, and when he finally shot a large doe, it ran headlong into the water and mud of the marsh before it fell. Dale had no choice but to go in after it.

It was fortunate that it was a weekend morning when he shot the deer. Even though the days were getting shorter, he had plenty of daylight to his advantage. What proved difficult was water and sinking mud that made it difficult to walk, let alone pull out a large deer that was literally, dead weight.

Having been a Boy Scout, Dale had tried to live by the motto, "to be prepared." He had a long rope with him that he tied to the doe. After he made his way to the most stable ground that he could find, he pulled the deer to him, and repeated the process until he made his way out of the marsh.

Cottonwood
By Kevin J. Curtis

It had been frightening at times, since he wasn't sure if he would get stuck in the mud. The thought of sinking to his death in the middle of the wildlife refuge was not a very pleasant one. Having a hunting partner would be a welcome thing.

This year, the weather had turned cold, and the fresh snow was a welcome sight when Dale and Sang reached the Wilkie unit of the Minnesota Valley National Wildlife Refuge. This was one of a few units on the refuge where hunting was allowed, though it was only open to bow hunting due to the close proximity to the cities.

The location was one of the things that Dale liked about it. Because of the close proximity to the city where he lived, it was easy to come and hunt for a few hours if that was all the time that he had available. There were no firearms hunters to be wary of, so Dale chose to wear camouflage clothing. There were also few people who ventured into this part of the refuge, especially off-trail and in the cold of late fall/early winter.

Dale parked his truck and he and Sang hiked out to an area that was bordered by the river, one of the lakes, and some woods. There was a large area of scrub brush and swamp, and it was perfect habitat for deer. The two hunters had already chemically masked their scent, and they settled in on small folding stools to wait for deer.

* * * *

Near the same place where Dale and Sang would hunt several generations later, another hunt had taken place. The two hunters were related by marriage, as the man whose name translated into English as "Red Deer," had taken his comrade, "Fishing Bird's" sister as his wife.

They were crouched low in the snow, waiting in ambush for deer that were feeding on the dried vegetation of the swamp. There were deer tracks and droppings in the

Cottonwood
By Kevin J. Curtis

area, and the two men figured that it was only a matter of time before they would have deer come through.

They made sure that they were upwind from the direction of their expected prey. Each man was armed with a wooden, short bow, expertly curved and tied with a bowstring made from sinew. They had arrows in hollow, wooden quivers that they wore across their backs. They each wore a warm deerskin robe, as these animals had hollow hair that was an excellent insulator against the cold and wind.

The arrows that the hunters had were made of straight willow branches. They had guide feathers on the shafts, and points made of chipped stone. The arrowheads were remarkably sharp, and this equipment was as accurate and deadly as one could get at this point in time. These men were highly skilled, and had created these weapons themselves.

* * * *

Dale looked at his watch. Only an hour had gone by. Even with his sophisticated equipment, sitting motionless was difficult, and he could feel the slight chill of the cold outside temperatures, slowly penetrating his gloves and boots. No matter what, he found it difficult to keep his hands and feet warm unless he was moving.

Sang sat motionless. He was excited by the prospect of shooting his first deer, yet he was a little bored. It had been over an hour now, and he wasn't sure how long they would have to wait. He was afraid to talk to his brother-in-law, because the sound of his voice might give away their position to any deer that might be close by.

Dale quietly opened his thermos, and took a drink of the hot coffee inside before sealing it back up and setting it back in his open backpack that was resting on the ground in front of him. He leaned over to Sang and whispered,

Cottonwood
By Kevin J. Curtis

"I'm going over that way a few yards. You stay here and we'll see what happens. If a deer comes, whoever is closest can shoot first."

Sang nodded, and Dale slowly moved across the new snow with his pack and bow, until he found a suitable place about fifty yards to Sang's left. Then the two settled back into waiting for deer.

* * * *

Red Deer was silent, but his hand signals told Fishing Bird that he intended to find a new location to wait out the deer. Fishing Bird understood that he was to remain where he was. By spreading out, they would increase the area of their ambush.

The wind was cold, and though they wore animal skins and furs, their clothes were well-made and they were accustomed to the cold and could squat motionless for hours at a time. This was their livelihood, and to fail as a hunter could mean starvation for their families.

Eventually, after crouching quietly for the entire morning, the two men heard a quiet rustling within the tall, dried vegetation of the marsh. A small group of deer were moving toward them. The two hunters remained silent and motionless, as the deer continued browsing on the dried plants and moved closer. The animals frequently lifted their heads and looked and listened intently for wolves, cougars and other predators that might be stalking them. As of yet, they had not caught scent of the two humans, though that could easily happen by a slight shift in the direction of the wind.

Each hunter had an arrow ready, as they waited for the moment between being discovered by their quarry and minimizing the distance needed to fire their arrows. Fishing Bird motioned with his fingers that he was eyeing the old buck that was closest to them. It was a large animal that

Cottonwood
By Kevin J. Curtis

would provide a good amount of meat, should they be able to kill it. Red Deer nodded once, and the two continued to wait patiently as the five animals in the group moved toward them and to the right.

    Finally, after waiting for what seemed to be a long time, Fishing Bird stood up from his hiding place to the right of Red Deer. At the same moment he stood, he fired an arrow into the old buck just as it realized he was there. The five deer all turned and ran in the other direction from where Fishing Bird was standing. The arrow was buried in the side of the buck, and it was obviously under distress.

    As the deer jumped across the expanse, Red Deer now rose from his position. While running away from Fishing Bird, the deer had headed directly toward the other hunter. Red Deer shot his arrow, which penetrated the chest of the old buck. The animal dropped to its knees and fought to regain its footing.

    Red Deer walked calmly toward the animal. In his hand he held a spear with a chipped stone point attached to the end. The deer was wide-eyed, knowing it was about to die. The hunter thrust the spear through the old buck's neck, and the lifeblood drained out of the animal, into the fresh snow.

    The keen eyes of the crows caught sight of the red-stained snow as the men quartered their prize, and ate the heart raw. They thanked the spirit of the deer for giving his life so that they could feed their families. As the two men hiked away through the snow with as much meat as they could drag and carry, the crows moved in to help themselves to the spoils.

* * * *

    After waiting for over two hours, Dale was considering calling off the hunt, except that he knew how badly and how determined Sang was to get a deer. The

Cottonwood
By Kevin J. Curtis

morning light had given way to midday, and though it was cloudy, Dale knew that dawn and dusk presented the best opportunities for success. He had always liked mornings, for the simple fact that finding a wounded deer and dragging it out of the marsh in the dark, presented hazards and difficulties that he would rather avoid.

Sang was also growing weary of the hunt, though he wanted to show Dale that he was not a quitter. As a result, the two men "toughed-it-out" for another half hour until they heard the sound of rustling in the dried marsh vegetation. The sound was quiet, but distinct and soon they noticed the forms of four deer traveling together in a group.

The buck's antlers had four points, but his body was large. He would not lose his antlers until later in the winter. With him, were three antlerless deer, likely does of varying ages and sizes. The two hunters kept still, except for readying their arrows. The first shot would be Sang's, as the deer were angling toward him.

The animals came closer, and Sang could feel his pulse quicken as he tried to determine how close he could allow the animals to come before he needed to react. Though he was a good hunter of small game, deer hunting was new to him and he now wished that the deer were heading toward Dale instead of him.

Despite his doubts, he focused on the mission of shooting his arrow into the heart of the buck that was moving toward him. The animals kept browsing on the dried plants and scanning the area with eyes and ears for danger. As Sang pulled back his bow, he placed the chest of the buck within his site and prepared to release the trigger on his compound bow. At that moment, something in the air startled the young buck and he stopped cold.

The buck fled away from Sang in a great bound as the hunter released his arrow. The cruel tipped projectile

Cottonwood
By Kevin J. Curtis

flew harmlessly past the four deer as they ran away in the other direction.

The fleeing animals were now headed almost directly at Dale as he quickly pulled back his bow and released his arrow. At dizzying speed, the four deer rushed past Dale, two on either side of him–as his arrow sailed into the cattail marsh where it was lost forever.

As the two men watched the deer run into the trees and out of sight, they shook their heads and walked toward each other to recount in excited voices, what had just happened. They were unsuccessful, today… but they would come back again soon.

Fortunately for these two modern-day hunters, this unsuccessful hunt would have no bearing on whether or not they were able to eat today. As they hiked back to Dale's truck, they made plans for their next hunt, and poured over the details of what had happened. They tried to analyze what they might have done differently, though the thrill of getting a shot off was still very much alive in them.

When they reached the truck, Dale opened it and the two men stowed their weapons and took off some of their outer clothing. They were feeling the chill of the weather, but knew that the truck's heater would soon be too hot for the gear they had been wearing.

On the way home, the two decided to stop by one of Dale's favorite, post-hunt locations. Inside of the bar and grill, the two hungry hunters enjoyed cheeseburgers and beers before continuing home.

Hunting had changed over time, and so had the hunters. The equipment was different, and the activity was now a sport, rather than a means of survival. Despite this, hunting was also a link to the past. It was no worse to take your meat from an animal that had run free in the wild, as it was to kill one that had been penned or caged for its entire life.

Cottonwood
By Kevin J. Curtis

Human beings are omnivorous and possess those qualities of both carnivores and herbivores. The eyes of a human point forward like those of a wolf or cougar, yet humans do not lap water like these animals, but tend to suck in water like horses, cattle and deer. Acknowledging your place in the ecosystem can put ethical hunting into perspective–despite the counter views of activists and vegetarians.

While Dale and Sang missed the chance to kill a deer today, they were now eating cheeseburgers and sitting in a warm bar, rather than lifting a couple of hundred pounds of dead deer into the truck.

Dale shoved his plate toward the bar. Half of his french-fries were uneaten, but he'd had enough. He dropped some money onto the counter to pay his tab, and he and Sang walked back to the truck to go home.

* * * *

Back in their winter village, Red Deer and Fishing Bird sat close to the small fire in the main lodge. The smell of cooking meat was in the air, and the dogs sat close by the doorway, to take advantage of any less-than-desirable pieces that might be cast in their direction. A young girl, one of Red Deer's daughters, refilled her father's drinking vessel with water that she had brought back from the creek.

The mood of the people was good. There was plenty to eat today. The bulk of the winter still lay ahead of them, but they had food stored and there were good hunters and plentiful game. The women were busily cooking and drying the meat and curing the hide of the buck. In this society, at this point in history, very little would go to waste.

Cottonwood
By Kevin J. Curtis

Chapter 26: Making Something from Nothing

Much time had passed, and the cottonwood tree had found favorable conditions. It had grown into a huge tree that was three feet wide at the base.[9] The inside of the tree was hollow and the cavity within had become home to numerous creatures over the years. It stood tall and its branches reached out wide. This tree, growing near the riverbank, was one of the monarchs of the bottomland forest.

He had left everything. He sold his house in Minneapolis, and left his government job to pursue a dream out east. When that dream didn't workout, he left the eastern seaboard and returned to the Midwest. He had never felt at home out east, but now, back in Minnesota, he had to rebuild his life.

Moving into his parents' basement at his age was embarrassing, though he was glad to be back, and they were glad to have him home. While he hadn't been away all that long, the fifteen hundred miles of distance had prevented all but one in-person visit.

He marveled at the irony. Years earlier, when he had finally graduated from college after attending part-time and working to pay his way through, there was a President George Bush and a war in Iraq. Now, years later, when he was once again struggling to recreate his life, there was yet again another President George (W.) Bush, and another war in Iraq. Each time, this also meant that the job market was depressed and good jobs were hard to find.

He had time on his hands, and he filled his days by going to the library and the Workforce Center. He would look for jobs and then write. He had an idea for a story that seemed like it had to be told. He spent his mornings engaged in writing and looking for work.

Cottonwood
By Kevin J. Curtis

  During those morning writing sessions, his book seemed to develop its own momentum. Sometimes he felt as if he were merely the conduit that the story flowed through. He was never quite sure where the novel would go and what would happen until he typed the words. Some of these sessions left him exhausted; yet he felt energized by his daily hikes in the bottomland forest.
  In the afternoons, he found himself most frequently hiking through the Minnesota River Valley. Though it was winter, he found it to be an excellent time to wander off the trail. There were no biting insects, and much of the usual soggy, sinking mud was frozen. The growth was down too, and there were few thorns or irritating plants to bother him.
  By early in the year 2004, he was spending nearly everyday in the wildlife refuge, exploring and keeping a record of it through his 35mm photography. By March of that year, after an e-mail inquiry to the manager of the wildlife refuge offering his services to help the refuge, he was called in by staff and given the title of *Volunteer Park Ranger.*
  After a brief orientation, he continued his solitary explorations of the wildlife refuge and its surrounding areas. Only now, he documented his journeys in writing, and sent the reports to the U.S. Fish & Wildlife staff. The many hours he volunteered turned into information for staff and funding from the federal government. Because he was on foot instead of driving a vehicle like the regular, paid staff, he traveled into areas and saw things that many of them didn't know about.
  He found owls, both Great Horned and Barred especially in the winter. With the leaves off of the trees, he could see them especially well. These spectacular birds usually saw him first, though, and often the view was of the owl flying away. Some days he got lucky and saw one in a tree. Once, on an early spring hike in the Wilkie unit of the

Cottonwood
By Kevin J. Curtis

Minnesota Valley Wildlife Refuge, he found a Great Horned Owl on her nest. Actually, it was probably formerly a hawk's nest, now being used by the owl.

As with most raptors, the female was larger than the male. He tried not to disturb the nesting bird, but the volunteer ranger quietly crept closer for a better look. The female didn't leave the nest, but the male was nearby. Smaller than his mate, he flew off into the distance.

The volunteer soon noticed that the big owls had a certain pattern that they adhered to when they saw him coming. The Great Horned Owls would launch themselves from the tree branch they were sitting on, and then go into a dive. A few feet from the ground, the bird would adjust its wings so that it would shoot forward and glide across the forest floor for a good distance. Then, suddenly, it would shoot back upward and find another branch to land on.

It was also on a winter hike in the Wilkie, that the volunteer found an eagle nest along the river. When he returned to check on it early in the spring, two eagles were there. The larger female was sitting on the nest. That summer, the two Bald Eagles raised a single eaglet. On one of his trips to view the young eagle, he saw no activity at the nest. It was late spring, and neither of the adult eagles was at the nest.

Curious, the volunteer went closer to investigate if there was any sign of the adult birds or of any newly hatched eaglets. Moments later he noticed the new eagle's head barely showing above the nest. Suddenly he saw the forms of two adult eagles coming at him. The parents had come home on the wing!

The female was screaming and swooped down within about fifteen feet[23] of the surprised ranger's head. The male also swooped in but not as close. The two birds flew large circles and then swooped again. The volunteer did what any good naturalist would do. Camera in hand, he

Cottonwood
By Kevin J. Curtis

snapped several pictures as he backed out, away from the tree containing the nest.

While close-up Bald Eagle sightings became commonplace for him, there was only one other time over the next couple of years that he was chased away by a ten-plus lb.[7] heavily armed bird. It was in the Long Meadow Lake Unit on the proposed (or undeveloped) State Trail. The volunteer knew that there was an eagle's nest on the other side of an area of young, dense trees.

He navigated through the tangle of trees toward the area where he thought the nest was. He originally intended to be close, but not too close once he broke cover. When he finally reached the edge of the young trees, he was near the edge of the lake beneath the larger trees. That was when a huge adult eagle swooped in. The volunteer backed up into the tangle of trees he had just emerged from. While it was unlikely the bird would actually attack him, the large talons and the feet of a Bald Eagle are thought to have approximately 400psi of pressure. He thought it prudent to not push his luck or stress out the bird.

Occasionally, the volunteer would feel frustrated by his position in life. He was searching for a job, and it seemed he was growing older without having the things he felt that he should have achieved by this point. It was about this time that the eagles came to his rescue.

While hiking in the Louisville Swamp unit of the Minnesota Valley National Wildlife Refuge, the volunteer found himself on a walking bridge, watching two eagles flying in the distance. The two birds were in the air, somersaulting and diving at incredible speeds. Through his spotting scope, he noticed the image getting larger as the birds were coming directly at him. He pulled the scope away from his eye, and the two birds sailed directly over his head, so close that he could hear the wind in their wings.

Copyright © 2008 by Kevin J. Curtis

Cottonwood
By Kevin J. Curtis

  The quiet sound was similar to that of a kite in the wind. The birds were not flapping their wings when they passed, but rather, they were gliding together at a tremendous speed. After they passed, with that sound still resonating inside of him, the volunteer decided right then and there, that he was truly blessed by some higher power, and that he was a very lucky man. Over the next couple of years, he found all nine of the active eagle nests on the refuge, and he was able to watch several of the young eaglets grow up.

  While he frequently saw the eagles sitting in the trees or flying overhead, he soon learned to rely on other means to find the birds. It was often the eagles' calls that alerted the volunteer ranger that they were nearby. That unmistakable shrill, metallic sound was often what would giveaway the location of these huge birds or their nests.

  One other telltale sign was the enormous quantity of white droppings beneath a favorite roost or one of the gigantic nests. The eagles' defecation was hard to miss, especially if they spent any time in the same place. Sometimes the volunteer joked that he found the nest in the Bloomington Ferry unit, "because of a lot of shit."

  The raptors were obvious favorites for him when he went hiking, and the volunteer saw several kinds. Two that he saw frequently, were Red-tailed Hawks, and Turkey Vultures. The vultures were only common during the warmer months, but during the summer of 2004, they were especially abundant.

  Once while off-trail in Louisville Swamp, a single vulture began circling low over the volunteer as he was returning from a rock formation that had Prickly Pear Cacti growing in it. Prickly Pear is the only cactus that can survive in Minnesota's climate. As he watched the vulture circle overhead, the volunteer called out, "I'm not dead

Cottonwood
By Kevin J. Curtis

yet!" As if it understood, the bird circled higher and then flew off.

One other time that summer, the volunteer went to the sanitary landfill in the city of Burnsville, near the boarder with Savage. He asked permission from the waste management company, to view the Turkey Vultures that congregated in large quantities near the top of the landfill. These birds found much to eat amidst the human garbage. The woman working in the office agreed to take him to the top of the mounds, and they jumped in a 4x4 pickup and went up.

The vultures shied away when the humans got too close, but never had the volunteer seen that many vultures at one time. Using his technique of counting ten, and then visualizing the amount of tens in the larger group, he decided that there were approximately sixty birds at the top.

One of his most interesting encounters with a Red-tailed Hawk occurred in the river valley along Nine-Mile Creek during the early winter of 2004. A young hawk appeared along the trail, sitting in a tree just above the volunteer's head. Knowing that the American Indians regarded the hawk as a messenger from the heavens, the volunteer asked the bird it if it had a message for him. The hawk flew off and then appeared two more times directly along the trail that the volunteer was following. Each time he asked the same question, and each time the bird flew off again. Eventually, the volunteer decided to find the answer within himself. He felt confident that this was what the bird had been sent to tell him.

Another notable bird encounter included the two Pileated Woodpeckers that showered him with woodchips as they hammered a tree above him near Nine-Mile Creek. There were many birds that came through, cormorants, Kingfishers, snow geese and migratory ducks such as

Cottonwood
By Kevin J. Curtis

Common and Hooded Mergansers and Common Goldeneyes.

During the late fall, there was a lake in Wilkie that was a favorite stopping place for migrating swans. There were Tundra (or Whistling) swans and Trumpeter Swans. One fall in 2005, the volunteer counted about three hundred swans in a lake in the Wilkie unit. He also noticed a few White-fronted geese.

Other animals he found, included, a large Common Snapping Turtle at the bottom of a small waterfall in East Wilkie. The waterfall was hard to get to because of the unstable ground. The mud would pull you down if you stepped in the wrong place. Under the areas that appeared stable, water ran beneath the ground and a person's weight would collapse the land above it. The volunteer negotiated the area by carefully walking along the edge of the stream. When he found the waterfall, he couldn't believe how beautiful it was. All around him were tall reeds and cattails. This small waterfall was beyond the view of anyone who was afraid to negotiate the terrain.

Also in this area of East Wilkie, he had two rather disturbing dog encounters. The first was when he found a large dog, possibly a greyhound that had been run over and dismembered by a train. The animal still had a collar and leash on it, and a metal pipe lay next to it as if someone had beaten it with the pipe and left it on the railroad tracks.

The second was when he found himself separated by Eagle Creek, from a huge black dog that appeared to have taken something down or possibly found a dead animal on the other side. The dog looked like a Presa Canario.[24] It was very large with short, black hair and a huge head. Eagle Creek is not wide, so the volunteer hurried past the area. While he had confrontations with other dogs in the wildlife refuge, he felt fortunate to never have seen this particular animal again.

Cottonwood
By Kevin J. Curtis

Over the next two years, the volunteer found many other kill sites and many dead animals. Once, in the Bloomington Ferry Unit, he found a medium sized skeleton in a tree. He also found other animals that had been killed by trains, including deer, opossums and a snapping turtle. Once, he found a deer that had apparently jumped from the Cedar Bridge, down into the Black Dog Preserve. The dead body lay broken on the ground below.

Sometimes there was only blood and fur, or blood and feathers to distinguish a kill-site. This was especially true in the winter, when the blood showed so well against the snow. Sometimes there were parts of bodies, or even entire carcasses. The volunteer had seen many deer carcasses while hiking in the river valley. Some were picked clean by coyotes. Others were still fresh. Sometimes all that was left was the gut-pile from a human hunter taking a deer. Most scavengers weren't interested in these gut-piles, since they contained half digested plant material. The small amount of animal matter was simply a large membrane and was apparently not too palatable to the larger scavengers.

As far as mammals, he saw numerous deer, opossums, rabbits, woodchucks, mink, beavers, muskrats and other animals. On occasion, he saw coyotes, foxes and raccoons. He also encountered numerous turtles, Garter Snakes, frogs, fish and insects.

The volunteer found signs of animals that were not easily seen. He saw slides and tracks of River Otters. He saw beaver dams and lodges and many burrows and nests. As far as nests, nothing was quite so grand as the nine active eagle nests he knew about, or the heron colony. During the winter, West Wilkie was open to the public. During the summer, it was closed because of a huge nesting colony of Great Blue Herons and Common Egrets. It was

Cottonwood
By Kevin J. Curtis

incredibly impressive, to see the hundreds of nests in the trees above when the leaves were gone in winter.

The volunteer soon learned to read the land. When traveling through the swamp, more than once he found himself over his head in grass, brush or reeds. He also sometimes found the water and mud getting deeper. Learning to read the land became invaluable in these situations.

He found that he could read the tree-line, to determine where to find safe passage. The living trees usually meant solid ground. Dead trees, such as the *ghost trees,* usually meant unstable ground or water. The ghost trees were dead trees that were still standing, and had usually succumbed to continuously wet ground. Often, it was beavers that caused this to happen when their dams caused flooding in an area that was previously dry. Certain types of plants preferred dryer conditions, and others grew right in the waters of the swamp. Knowing the difference could lead you out of the potentially deadly muck.

While hiking the swampy areas with a stick to test the ground to see if it could support his weight, the volunteer imagined a prehistoric man doing the same thing centuries earlier. To such a man, he surmised, such a skill would be incredibly valuable–though it was now all but lost to modern people who spent most of their lives on paved roads.

Learning to read the land was something that came by spending time in the bottomland. It came by developing an intimate knowledge of this environment and its features. The seasons changed these features, and the industrious beavers could also change the land/water ratio of an area literally overnight.

The river valley was also prone to flooding. Many times The volunteer had hiked five or more miles[25] just to find a bridge or levee underwater. This usually meant one

Cottonwood
By Kevin J. Curtis

of two things. Either he would have to cross through the water, which could be uncomfortable or even dangerous, or he would need to turn around and hike all the way back to where he had come from.

This was just one of the gambles that one had to take if he were to hike through all of the many areas or the wildlife refuge. Even after returning home wet and tired, the volunteer always felt it was worthwhile because of all of the land and water features, and the diverse animal life that he was able to see.

Perhaps even more impressive than the abundance of animal life, was the huge diversity of plant life. It seemed that each unit of the refuge and each section of the river valley had its own plants and features. There were pines growing in some areas, while deciduous trees dominated the other landscapes. There were unbelievable numbers of smaller plants as well. One thing that truly impressed the volunteer was the diversity of wildflowers.

Each unit of the refuge had different wildflowers that dominated the area. The time of year also had its own set of dominant flowers. The prairie section of Rapids Lake boasted such beautiful specimens as Butterfly Weed, Prairie Smoke, Black-eyed Susan and more. Down the ravines in the forest, there were Columbines and Honey Suckle.

Black Dog Preserve was home to brilliant flowers such as Prairie Blazing Star, Rough Blazing Star, Cup Plant, Prairie Clover and Bottle Gentian. Many areas in the bottomland contained Gray-headed and Green-headed Coneflowers, Daisy Fleabane, Wild Bergamot, lilies, Water lilies, Arrowhead, iris, Lead Plant, White Snakeroot, Morning Glory, Marsh Marigolds, milkweed, Jack-in-the-Pulpit, thistles, anemones, Spotted-knapweed, Joe-Pye Weed, vervain, phlox, bellflowers and various lobelias and

Copyright © 2008 by Kevin J. Curtis

Cottonwood
By Kevin J. Curtis

asters. There were also less abundant flowers such as Turtlehead and American Lotus.

Different times of the growing season brought different flowers. Blood Root was among the first to bloom. Vast numbers of other flowers followed, with Cup Plants, Western Ironweed and coneflowers blooming late in the summer.

The different refuge units had different terrain, such as the ravines in Rapids Lake, the bluffs in Long Meadow Lake, the pines in Wilkie and the rock formations in Louisville Swamp. All of the units had either ponds, marshes, lakes, the river, creeks, streams or usually some combination of several of these.

During the summer months, there were also a number of irritating plants and insects. There were nettles growing under the trees in the shade. These grew quite tall, and they had tiny spines that created a very painful itch. There were a couple of times during the heat of summer, when the volunteer was wearing shorts but still couldn't resist going off trail. The nettles were the single most excruciating irritants at those times.

Once, while in Wilkie, he was "stung" so many times by these nettles, that his legs were weeping blood. The plants "painted the blood across his skin until his legs became a crimson color. The itch was unbelievable, but the volunteer knew that he couldn't scratch or it would become worse. He soon found that after about ten minutes of *extreme* discomfort, the itch would start to dissipate.

There were other thorns and burrs. The wild roses, raspberries and a few other plants delivered painful, tearing wounds when they tore through the skin. Sometimes they would go through clothing too. There was also an abundance of poison ivy, which could look very different, depending on whether it was growing in sun or in shade. There were also numerous burrs and seedpods that stuck to

Cottonwood
By Kevin J. Curtis

skin, hair and clothing in incredible numbers. These were especially bad in the late summer and fall.

Of course, the insect pests were present in the warmer months. The mosquitoes were in great abundance due to all of the water in the area. There were occasions where despite having protective clothing and insect repellent, the volunteer could literally wipe these insects from his body.

Some of the more notable animal sightings that the volunteer had, included walking within a few feet of wild turkeys in the Long Meadow Lake unit, having a coyote cross his path in Black Dog Preserve, two mink fighting over a Garter Snake, and being followed by deer. The deer were curious, and seemed to be following him as the volunteer walked off the trail near Long Meadow Lake.

Other interesting sightings included the raccoon who was along the river's edge, another, baby raccoon in a tree at The Bloomington Ferry unit and a baby woodchuck, that charged the volunteer as he tried to pass it on the proposed state trail. There was also a rather large snapping turtle that reminded the volunteer of a military tank as it turned to face him. There was a carp that crossed a flooded road in Wilkie, and beavers swimming through the flooded woods.

When coming out of Wilkie or Rapids Lake after hiking off trail, there were times when the volunteer removed approximately fifty wood ticks from himself before entering his car. He generally found about ten or twelve more later when he got home.

Another pest during hot weather hikes, were the deerflies. These insects were relentless, with sometimes a couple of dozen circling at once. Periodically these flies would land and bite. They could deliver a painful bite and they were very quick. The volunteer would sometimes catch them in the air by grabbing blindly around his head.

Cottonwood
By Kevin J. Curtis

These captured flies were usually tossed aside after "losing" a wing. There were other smaller flies that would bite as well.

The water contained leaches, and crossing a flooded area could allow these small animals to take hold of bare skin. These were just a few of the many "biohazards" in the bottomland forest and marshes.

Other hazards included the garbage left behind by humans. There were bottles, cans and old, rusty barrels. There were old appliances, broken glass, barbed wire, automobile skeletons and some garbage that may have been leftover from the process of making drugs such as methamphetamines.

In winter, there were frozen lakes and ponds to cross. This could be risky, however, as there was often moving water in the area. There were trees to climb, rock ledges to climb, unstable marsh bogs to try to cross, and ravines to explore. One ravine in Rapids Lake had an eerie combination of bones and clothing at the bottom. The volunteer added all of these findings to his reports that he mailed in to the refuge staff.

There were some old buildings off trail in the Chaska unit and Wilkie, and two old farms in Louisville Swamp that had buildings or foundations still intact. These old, stone buildings were a reminder that people had once farmed this floodplain.

Other reminders of farm activity included the remnants of farm machinery. There were parts of tractors, wagons, old wheels and plowing equipment. Off trail in Wilkie, there was an old disc. The disc had been used to breakup the lumps in the soil of a farm field. This one was lodged between two trees–one being a huge Silver Maple. The steel farm implement was slowly being crushed and broken by the strength of the trees growing and pushing against it.

Cottonwood
By Kevin J. Curtis

Occasionally, the volunteer would bring someone with him on his hikes. More often than not though, he was alone in the woods. Sometimes during hunting season, he would spot a hunter in a tree stand or breaking cover up ahead. In winter, he would sometimes see the tracks of a hunter. When this occurred, he generally tried to hurry through the area or hike wide of the hunter's position.

Out there, alone, the woods and marshes could sometimes have a spooky feel to them. There were ghosts out there. These weren't the kind of spirits that jump out at you like in the movies. They were the people who had lived and died in these wild areas over thousands of years.

White culture was relatively new to the area, though the remnants of the stone buildings that remained might be hundreds of years old. The American Indians had walked these same woods for thousands of years, and sometimes, the volunteer felt as if they were still there.

He had learned that ghosts didn't usually stare him in the face so much as they could be felt by his soul. Other times, it was that figure in the corner of his eye that was almost out of his field of vision. There it was plain as day, and when he tried to focus on it, it was gone.

One such apparition appeared while the volunteer was hiking into the Rapids Lake unit of the wildlife refuge one morning. Across the meadow just inside of the tree-line, he noticed an American Indian in full traditional regalia. The man stood watching as the volunteer ranger moved toward the ravines to climb down to the lake.

Just about the time that the volunteer recognized the warrior, the Indian decided that this visitor posed no threat to the land, and he disappeared into the forest. The vision had been fleeting, though it felt real. When the volunteer entered the woods at the spot where he saw the ancient spirit, there were no tracks and no sign of a flesh-and-blood human.

Cottonwood
By Kevin J. Curtis

    While he put his life back in order over the next two years, the volunteer explored the bottomland forest extensively. Often, he would return home after several hours, tired, dirty and hungry. He felt useful when he reported to the refuge staff about what he saw on these hikes. He also felt good when he was tired and sore from an exhausting hike. Eventually, as civilized life set-in, such as when he began working two jobs and purchased a new home, he found that he was able to spend less time in the bottomland forest and marshes.

    Though less frequently, he still enjoyed hiking in the wildlife refuge when he found the time. He knew the area so well, that it was always interesting to see the way things had changed due to linear time, or because of the seasons.

    Over time, the volunteer had found the best areas to locate fruit such as wild grapes, raspberries and mulberries. He used this fruit to make homemade wines. Having also been a beer maker, the volunteer enjoyed creating fine wines from the fruit of the river valley. It was not always easy to find or pick though, and he was often rather covetous of when he would open one of these special bottles of wine.

    In order to get the raspberries, he had to go late in June and wear protective clothing–including a mosquito net around his head. The raspberries were usually in a tangle and the vines had sharp thorns on them. Once, while picking wild Black Raspberries in the Rapids Lake unit, he found some high-quality fruit growing up, around a huge fallen tree. The volunteer climbed up and walked along the tree trunk picking berries.

    At one point, the raspberry thorns stuck into his pant legs, and the vines "hog-tied" him. Up on the log about four feet[13] above the ground, he realized that he was going to fall! He went down, crashing through the

Cottonwood
By Kevin J. Curtis

raspberries and branches until he hit the forest floor. When he realized that he wasn't impaled by anything, and no bones were broken, he began trying to pickup his fruit, which had fallen out of his container that was held by a strap around his shoulder.

The raspberries were soft, and the dirt and leaves on the ground prevented him from recovering all of the lost fruit. Therefore, it is plain to see that this was not an easy way to get a bottle of wine.

The prime area for picking wild grapes was best accessed by bicycle. This meant a long ride down into the valley and an excruciating ride back up… up out of the river valley, loaded down with grapes. The fruit also contained many seeds, and it took a significant amount to make enough fruit juice for a batch of wine. Still, after adding enough honey to compensate for the tartness of the grapes, a really good wine/mead could be made.

On one fine spring day, the volunteer decided to hike out into the bottomland forest after work. He passed the swamp, and saw the ducks and geese. There were Great Blue Herons and Common Egrets. Above his head, he noticed a shadow pass over. When he looked up into the sunlit sky, there was a large Red-tailed Hawk sailing overhead.

The hike brought him to a huge cottonwood tree. The day was warm, and mosquitoes were not yet in season. He decided to sit on the ground and lean against this fabulous old tree to rest. He looked up at the cloudless sky, and then closed his eyes. Before long, he was dozing off.

Leaning back, with his head against the tree, he could feel the tough bark through his cap. The tree was old, more than twice his age. It seemed a comfortable place to rest. This land, this tree, all that was here seemed tied to a history that was obscured by time.

Cottonwood
By Kevin J. Curtis

The volunteer wondered if others had leaned against this tree. He thought about the animals and the native people who have come and gone. What had happened here? What residual energy existed here in this place, and inside of this giant tree?

Somewhere nearby, he could hear the pounding of a woodpecker. The ducks were calling to each other in the marsh. In the distance, the scream of the Red-tailed Hawk rang through the valley. He lay there for several minutes before standing up and brushing himself off.

He saw the beer can nearby. He was definitely not the only one who had been here. A few steps more and he found an old whiskey bottle. Before he made it back to the trail, he passed an old tire, a rusty barrel and several more cans and bottles. One difference between his visit and that of some of the other people, who had been there, was that he only left behind footprints, and a deep appreciation for the natural state of things.

As time went on, the volunteer found himself more occupied with work, family and friends. He went less frequently into his beloved bottomland forest. As time continued on, however, others also found solitude and wonder in the river valley.

As the living are only visitors within the linear reach of time, the valley itself showed its superiority as it continued on its way toward a new millennia.

Cottonwood
By Kevin J. Curtis

Chapter 27: Epilogue

The Minnesota Valley National Wildlife refuge is about 10 miles south of downtown Minneapolis. Established in 1976 as a habitat for birds and wildlife threatened by development, its true reason for being (largely) spared from human alteration is the fact that it keeps the surrounding cities safe from flooding.

Spanning much of the land surrounding the Minnesota River from Fort Snelling State Park to the cities of Jordan and Carver to the west, the refuge has eight land units, 14,000 acres and stretches some thirty-four miles. The original visitor center is located near the Mall of America in Bloomington, Minnesota. A second visitor center was opened in 2008, in the Rapids Lake unit near Carver, Minnesota. The Minnesota Valley National Wildlife Refuge also manages a fourteen county Wetland Management District (WMD). Most of these areas are open to the public, as is the refuge itself.

The refuge and the land around it have a long history. The wilderness that remains intact, gives us a glimpse of the Minnesota that existed when the American Indians dominated the landscape before the first white explorers arrived.

Though much has changed since then, one can still travel into the refuge and hike on trails that exist between the wild state of things, and the development that has come along by human intervention. At times, though minutes from the downtown areas, it is possible to become immersed in the natural world. This area has become an important recreational resource, especially where it is adjacent to lands preserved by the Minnesota Department of Natural Resources.

Cottonwood
By Kevin J. Curtis

Are we Gods or Bugs?

In the scheme of the world, there is much debate about our importance. In the past, nuclear war was a frightening prospect, because "we could blow up the whole world!" Could we actually destroy the planet, or would we just affect global changes that would destroy humanity and several other species–while the world just continued on without us?

No doubt, we humans have affected great changes on the planet. Just a few centuries ago, life was very different. People had to grow, hunt and barter for food. They also had to carry water. They had to cut wood to heat their homes that they likely had to build themselves. Today, we buy food at the grocery store, buy houses with money from working jobs, and we have electricity, water/sewer, and (at least where I live) in the Midwest, natural gas piped in to heat our homes.

When I hike the Minnesota Valley National Wildlife Refuge lands, I see that there are high-voltage lines spanning the area above, gas lines beneath the ground, and there is a huge power-plant at Black Dog. Black Dog was the name of an American Indian chief who once lived at the site, but now the name applies to the power-plant, the lake and the road between the two.

The power-plant allows for the production of electricity that is diverted and wired directly into our homes. This allows for a variety of lights and appliances that were not available in the past few centuries. This plant burns huge quantities of coal, which produces emissions. The resulting heat also causes heat-pollution to Black Dog Lake, as the plant uses the waters to cool its systems. As a result, certain fish, plants and animals cannot live in the waters, while others congregate there in the winter because it never entirely freezes over.

Cottonwood
By Kevin J. Curtis

    This, perhaps, demonstrates that people do have a major impact on the environment, usually disadvantageous to everyone, except for the comfort level of human beings. One can use the analogy of bacteria in a Petri-dish, polluting their environment until they die in their own waste. This could be humanity's fate at some point in the future.

    One thing we do know is that we have made changes in the world, and in the Minnesota River Valley, where the Black Dog power-plant is located. Still, the natural environment, the plants and the animals, hold on and some even thrive. Of course, we should remember that bears, wolves, cougars, elk and bison once roamed these areas, and they are for the most part, long gone. That said, there are still deer, coyotes, raccoons, lots of birds and wildflowers still in abundance.

    Our national emblem, the Bald Eagle, made a remarkable comeback after efforts were enacted to save this unique species of raptor from extinction. Unfortunately, other, less charismatic species do not enjoy the same level of public support. Their fates are more perilous.

    So in the end, as we consider global warming, are humans affecting serious and harmful changes on the world that will cause catastrophic events? Or, could it be that we are merely fooling ourselves, as a greater and grander series of natural forces follow their own patterns that have occurred over billions of years while humans were still evolving into the egomaniacs that we have become?

Cottonwood
By Kevin J. Curtis

About Cottonwoods

    Cottonwood trees are in so many ways, extremely impressive. That is, if they aren't growing in your yard. The average city lot is not nearly large enough to support the size that such a tree can grow to. Those who plant this tree because it is quick growing, may be sorry they did after it matures. Cottonwoods are also rather easily broken by strong winds–since they are softwoods. The loss of a single large branch, could be devastating if your house were underneath.

    In the Minnesota River Valley, I have found cottonwoods that are absolutely enormous. These trees are not generally long-lived, though they might be quite massive by age sixty, and rarely live to the century mark. One anomaly of this is the *Balmville Cottonwood,* of New York State. A core sample taken by a Harvard Scientist indicated that the tree began its life about 1699AD, and was still alive (though obviously at the end of its existence) in the early twenty-first century.

    Cottonwoods develop enormous trunks and seem to be relatively shallow rooted, as I have often seen them uprooted and tipped over from strong winds and flooding. These trees are usually hollow inside when they mature, and provide birds, animals and insects with a good source of shelter.

    One image that I have of a cottonwood, deviates drastically from the others. While I was visiting *White Sands National Monument* in New Mexico, I found a much smaller tree than I was used to,–though it was gnarled and had developed a unique character, due to life in the desert.

    I found this tree while hiking on the sand dunes in one hundred plus degree Fahrenheit heat (37.78 Celsius). The short hike I took was difficult due to the heat and the fact that the water within my body seemed to be removed

Cottonwood
By Kevin J. Curtis

into the surrounding air within a very short span of time. I drank the entire contents of my water bottle, and was ready to use the air conditioner in my car when I finished hiking. Still, growing in the sun baked, white sand dunes, along with a number of yucca plants, was a cottonwood tree. How very interesting, I thought, that this tree was able to survive in this desert, when the cottonwoods that I was familiar with grew in the Minnesota River Valley in soil that was generally damp.

   The cottonwoods are resilient, and have even been used to make things such as furniture, due to characteristics of taking stain well and not splitting when being nailed. Often, however, these trees are viewed negatively by those who have seen them overtake a city landscape, or by anyone who has had to coexist with one in a suburban yard. Aside from the fact that these trees are short-lived and can grow to enormous proportions, there is yet a more sinister aspect to them as far as human beings are concerned. The trademark "cotton" that houses the tree's seeds, and floats them on the wind, is usually unwelcome as it accumulates in yards and on window screens.

   I must admit, my appreciation for the cottonwoods began when I saw these trees growing in the river bottoms. The sheer size of them is something that can't be denied or ignored. My continued exposure to these magnificent trees as I hiked the Minnesota River Valley, is no doubt, the reason that they have become the anchor for my novel. While people, animals and events may come and go quickly, the cottonwoods bear witness to all of it.

Kevin J. Curtis

Cottonwood
By Kevin J. Curtis

Endnotes:

[1] 90 Feet equals 27.43 Meters

[2] 5 Feet equals 1.52 Meters

[3] 2.5 Feet equals 0.76 Meters

[4] 20 feet is equal to 6.10 meters

[5] 1 inch is equal to 2.54 centimeters

[6] 1 foot is equal to 0.30 meters

[7] 40 acres is equal to 0.16 square kilometers

[8] 10 lbs. is equal to 4.54 kilograms

[9] 7 feet is equal to 2.13 meters

[10] 3 feet is equal to 0.19 meters

[11] *noun*: any of a phylum (Arthropoda) of invertebrate animals (as insects, arachnids, and crustaceans) that have a segmented body and jointed appendages, a usually chitinous exoskeleton molted at intervals, and a dorsal anterior brain connected to a ventral chain of ganglia - *source*– Merriam-Webster online

[12] 6 feet is equal to 1.83 meters

[13] A long tube-like organ used to drink with

[14] 4 feet is equal to 1.22 meters

Copyright © 2008 by Kevin J. Curtis

Cottonwood
By Kevin J. Curtis

[15] 5 pounds is equal to 2.27 kilograms. 10 pounds is equal to 4.54 kilograms.

[16] Main Entry: **spo·ro·cyst**
Pronunciation: -"sist
Function: *noun*
Etymology: International Scientific Vocabulary
1: a case or cyst secreted by some sporozoans to sporogony; *also*: a sporozoan encysted in such a case.
2: a saccular body that is the first asexual reproductive form of a digenetic trematode, develops from a miracidium, and buds off cells from its inner surface, which develop into. Rediae - *source*– Merriam-Webster online

[17] 34 miles equals 54.72 kilometers

[18] Main Entry: **at·latl**
Pronunciation: 'ät-"lä-t[&]l
Function: *noun*
Etymology: Nahuatl *ahtlatl*
: a device for throwing a spear or dart that consists of a rod or board with a projection (as a hook) at the rear end to hold the weapon in place until released - *source*– Merriam-Webster online

[19] Smudge - **3** : to smoke or protect by means of a smudge *intransitive verb- source*– Merriam-Webster online

[20] 55 miles-per-hour equals 88.51 kilometers-per-hour

[21] 90 lbs. is equal to 40.82 kilograms

[22] 2 miles is equal to 3.22 kilometers

Cottonwood
By Kevin J. Curtis

[23] 15 feet is equal to 4.57 meters

[24] Presa Canario is also known as the Canary Island Fighting Dog.

[25] 5 miles is equal to 8.05 kilometers

Sources

The Prehistoric Peoples of Minnesota / Elden Johnson.
by Johnson, Elden.
St. Paul, MN : Minnesota Historical Society Press, 1988.
Call #: R977.6 J63

Minnesota Valley National Wildlife Refuge
<http://www.fws.gov/Midwest/MinnesotaValley/>

Minnesota Historical Society <http://www.mnhs.org/>

Bloomington Historical Society
<http://www.bloomingtonhistoricalsociety.org/>

Minnesota Conservation Volunteer
Minnesota Department of Natural Resources
500 Lafayette Road
St. Paul, MN 55155-4046

Cottonwood
By Kevin J. Curtis

About the author,

Kevin J. Curtis has a BA in English from the University of Minnesota. A lifetime writer, Kevin writes music, poetry, short stories and has two finished novels. Curtis lives in Minnesota with his wife Neng. He works in technology at an alternative high school. Kevin also volunteers as a park ranger in the Minnesota Valley National Wildlife Refuge. His first novel is called "He Who Goes First."